SINGSONG

# SINGSONG

MARTIN KEAVENEY

PENNILESS PRESS PUBLICATIONS

www.pennilesspress.co.uk/books

*Published by*
*Penniless Press Publications 2024*

**ISBN** 978-1-913144-61-6

*Cover: Mist at Lough Owel (Paul Butler).*

To Michael

# CONTENTS

## Publication History

'The Hunter'. *Crannog.* Issue 50 (Spring 2019): 55-60. Print.

'Jargon Wine'. *The Crazy Oik.* Issue 44 (Winter 2020): 92-98. Print.

'The Walker'. *The Writing Disorder*. Issue 41 (Spring 2020): Online.

'The Mourning'. *The Taborian.* Issue VIII (Summer 2024): Online.

'Dawn Chorus'. *Vassar Review*. Issue 9 (2024): 6-10 Print.

'Singsong'. *The Eunoia Review.* (April 2024): Online.

'The Viewing'. *Commuter Lit*. (April 2024): Online.

# DAWN CHORUS

She's not exactly good-looking. Not the way I'd have thought
good-looking was supposed to be when I was going to school.
She hasn't got big round eyes and film-star thick lips. Some
might even say she is plain. But the day I saw her down at the
Texaco, as I was sitting in my car on the forecourt at 8am,
waiting for the bakery van to arrive with the fresh cream and
jam doughnuts from the night shift, the strands of her black
hair falling by the right side of her face, covering one eye, one
cheek, half of her mouth, a helmet on the seat of the bike, her
pumping air into the front wheel by the air compressor in the
services area, her leathers turning silver in the sunlight, I got
pure disturbed. I've been disturbed since. It's following me
around, like a chorus in my head, the memory of the reflection
in her eyes. The delicate way she glided back on the glove
when she was finished.

I zoom in but the resolution is not that detailed. The
image becomes lost in pinpricks of colour. She could have
picked a better camera for her Facebook profile. I found her
through the 'Bikers West' group page. But she was riding
alone the day I saw her. Maybe she rides alone a lot. There's
not much on her personal page. A few things about the bike.
It's a Suzuki RG 125cc. She likes ice cream. She dislikes
tartan kilts and men's sandals. I like ice cream. I don't wear
tartan kilts or sandals. Good start. I suppose she could be just
making it up. But she looked genuine. In the photo, she looked
true. And now I have a plan.

The microwave pings. I take out my plate with my
Elvis apron. Bacon and cabbage and potatoes. Grandmother
used to cook it seven days a week. It would be on the table
when we'd call in from the herding. One o'clock on the dot.
Later herself and Grandfather would have pog, breadcrusts

soaked in tea and six spoons of sugar, with a boiled egg. There wouldn't be much talk. TV plugged in at the wall for the Angelus and the news. Plugged out again straight after. I used to wish they'd leave it on for *Home and Away*. They'd go straight to bed at seven. One single room each side of the kitchen. I liked it down there. I still do, even though there's weeds growing in the windows now.

I get a glass of milk and sit at the table. I scroll through her account. She doesn't post much. Only the odd thing about the bike or the Bikers' Group. A meeting next week, a rally at the end of the year. She could be married for all I know. But I don't think so. She had a kind of lost look that day at the Texaco. I don't know much about bikes. I'll have to learn.

I forgot to get YR sauce in Aldi. I was distracted after I saw her. I'm annoyed. I stare at the steaming dinner for a while. There's nowhere open out here in the country now. Not much open anywhere at this time of day. I should have got a flat in town years ago. Shuffling around this place in the middle of nowhere. Might suit her though. Living amongst the thicket, the brambles, the crawling ivy. She looks like one that could go for the wild.

Grandmother wouldn't have YR, nor any other sauce. But I didn't mind then. Square of butter yellowed onto the peeled steaming spuds, shot of salt, leaves of cabbage cooked with the bacon.

I get it all down anyway. I pull out the Christmas Cake from the press. They started selling it again last week. I cut four slices and make a mug of milky tea. A couple of birds are chirping out in the Beeches. I wonder would she like the sound of them early in the morning, us looking out the window, her in her skin, under the sheets beside me. Might get a feeding tray out there for them. I heard it's good to watch them nibble on the grain. I can hear the solid sound from their little throats. That's a good singer, one that can carry a note strong in the exhale. The sound gets through to you, you feel the music of it. All the birds can do that, but not all the people. But I don't know much about music.

I look out past the trees, to the green fields. I often think about taking back the land and farming it myself. Seems a sin to be letting someone else work it. But I was never any good with animals. The rent keeps me going all right.

Dawn will be at 4.34am today, according to the internet forecast. Grandmother told me the Dawn Chorus always starts with one bird twittering. Then, after a while, another joins the first. Eventually a big group of them are at it, their little lungs puffing, singing together in harmony. Must be that they can't resist chirping together in the glory of the new dawn. That's what Grandmother told me. But all I've ever heard is a couple of them tweeting like they are now, out in the Beeches. There's never any chorus. Grandmother said the dawn is a magical time. Spiritual powers become available to a man at that part of the day. It's funny that's when they execute him.

Great sweetness in the cake. I can feel the sugar warming my blood. Tastes the same as wedding cake, more or less. All in the way it is ordered, whether it is festive or marking a union. All in the way it is finished off.

I shiver as I look at the screen again, see her profile and me thinking about wedding cake. That must be the mystical properties of the dawn at work.

It reminds me of my plan. I search for 'Love Spells'. Eighty million results. The first few pages are spells that don't cost anything. But Grandmother used to say anything free was always too dear in the finish. So I skip all those. I get to a site with a 'Deluxe Love Chant.' This comes with a bonus spell for growing extra spicy tomatoes. It costs $1200. It takes six months to work. I scroll to another site. It has a spell called 'Angel Heart'. This one requires two kilos of garden clay. It costs $600 and you have to supply the muck yourself.

I keep searching. Internet is gone awful slow. I tap my fingers, looking out at the Beeches. The tweeting has stopped. The next website I visit has a warning in red letters about love spells that use clay or sellers that offer bonus spells that promise to improve the taste of vegetables. They would be 'Spurious Goods', according to 'The Spellmaster.' He has a special offer of a 'Cupid Spell' for $50. The Spellmaster looks honest enough, even if he is only a smiley cartoon drawing. I'm getting tired of looking. I get out my debit card and buy it. I don't believe in magic, but maybe I could turn my mind around. This spell only takes 12 hours if I follow the instructions. It's not long to wait.

I check to see if The Spellmaster has sent me an email receipt. But the internet is not working at all now. I go to the windowsill and find the phone bill with the 24-hour helpline number.

They answer straight away. 'Hello! Thank you for contacting us. The 24-hour helpline is available 24 hours a day. However, all of our operators are unavailable at the moment. Please hold or press the hash key to leave a message.' The voice sounds very happy. I start to feel happy too. Classical music starts playing. It's nice. I turn on the mirror on my phone. After nearly five decades, I'm still not a bad catch. Chubbiness keeps wrinkles away. Fully bald, but I've no remedy for that. I smile at the screen. Teeth might need shining up. I wait five minutes. I press the hash key and leave a message.

My appointment is at ten. I am in the waiting room at quarter past nine. The girl at the desk tells me Noel the dentist isn't in yet. There is no one else waiting. I might be the only patient he has today. I'm not sure how long he has a surgery in the town. You don't hear much about dentists starting a practice. There's no official opening. Speeches, applause, balloons. Suits and flowing dresses. Music. Cake. It's not a thing to get excited about. A new dentist coming to the town. Like a hotel or a swimming pool. Or a shoe shop. Unless you are the dentist or his mother.

She has posted something in her account. Seems she will be in town later. She is getting the chrome adjusted on her bike. She might use the garage at the back of the Texaco. I'll go there after I see Noel and wait. I'll be fit for nothing else if I have to get one or two out. All that Christmas Cake. It could be time to pay for it. Might have to get them all out. False teeth then like Grandmother. Her mouth fell in when she wasn't wearing the dentures. You'd see it if you called early in the morning. The strange shape of her face. One half of it fallen in. Never bothered me though. It was always quiet in their house. I liked it.

I get an email with the spell attached as I wait. The Spellmaster thanked me for my custom and wished me the best. I download the spell and open it on my phone. It's only a few lines. I get annoyed. I was expecting a bit more for $50. A picture or a few diagrams at least. But I've paid now. I have to get three sand pebbles and do some kind of meditation. I don't know what sand pebbles are. I wonder if they are marbles. I have a set in a drawer out in the shed. We used to have great games of marbles years ago.

I'm told that Noel has arrived. The girl leads me into the surgery. The surgery assistant is a girl too. Classical music plays. It's the same as the phone company track. Must be specially for waiting. I don't mind the sound. I don't know much about classical music or orchestras. All of them trained musical brains, all following the same song sheet, each playing their individual instrument. Like the birds flying to the Beeches in a perfect triangle. Same when they sing the Dawn Chorus, all chirping together. If I could ever get to hear it.

Noel comes out of what I guess is his office. It's more like a booth, with a little plastic window facing the surgery.

Grandmother had a window like that in the kitchen where you could see into a hall and the front door that they never opened. It had foggy yellow glass each side. I used to think it was funny, a window inside a house. It even had curtains, lace and a window board.

Noel's booth is about the size of a telephone box. You don't see many of them now. The door is broke-off the one in Main Street, the hood for the head cracked. Graffiti on the scratched wooden panel. It's like an antique, the big blue handset, the dead grey buttons. Not many even know what they are these days. I must be ageing. I used to ring a girl from one every Sunday. It was the last year of school. I was smoking then, my brown boots with yellow lacers pressed against the Perspex at the bottom, the dial tone buzzing in my ear, me wondering would she ever answer. Her waiting in another phone box twenty miles away. I sometimes think of the shampoo smell in her curls when we'd dance at the disco.

Noel fits on his gloves. He's much rougher than she was with the leather mitts after she was finished that day by the air compressor in the services area at the Texaco. Noel stretches the rubber around his hands, snaps the tips off his fingernails. I wonder is he getting ready to do a big job. I get nervous. 'How are we today?' he says. I've had my mouth stretched open since I lay on the chair, so I don't answer. He sits beside me and leans over. He checks my teeth with a tiny mirror on a stick. He hums as he works. He says all my teeth are fine. I ask him to check again. He humours me but they are still all good.

I'm surprised, I say. I tell him I eat a lot of cake. 'What type of cake?' he wants to know. He nods when I say Christmas Cake. He asks me how often I brush my teeth. Twice a day, I tell him. I mouthwash after. I change my brush every month. 'Good man!' he says then. He still wants to give my teeth his special type of cleaning anyway. It's €50 extra,

14

but it's probably as much use to me as the spell. Maybe even more use.

The assistant gives me a pair of plastic glasses to wear. Noel uses a whizzing electric brush. The head on it is much smaller than on mine. It glides over my gums. It hits my nerves in places and my eyes water. I yelp once. Noel doesn't take any notice and keeps brushing.

He is humming again. He was humming as well when he came out of the booth. He must be happy at his work. Strange job. Operating on mouths all day. In some countries, dentists aren't allowed to do jury duty. I was wondering why. I might ask him about that before I go. Maybe if they are judging a case and the dentist doesn't agree with the verdict. Eleven says 'Not Guilty' and Noel says 'Guilty'. *Twelve Angry Men* and all that. The suspect is released and Noel sees the man he thinks is guilty every day passing by the surgery. One day the man comes in to get a tooth out. Then Noel has miniature drills and hammers in the suspect's mouth. Syringes full of drugs. Noel working on a suspect he believes has got away with murder. Makes sense when you think about it. Even if Noel hums a lot. They probably should ban barbers too. Standing over your eyes with a scissors. It's asking for trouble. Lucky my hair fell out years ago. Don't have to worry about that one.

On the way home, I pass the old telephone booth. I stop and go in, look at the graffiti, the ancient instructions panel, the smashed door hinge. Some people pass by and glance over. Even someone standing in one now is unusual. The last night I rang the girl with the curls, it was her friend that was on the line. She told me her friend wouldn't be answering any more on Sunday evenings. Or any other evening. She wasn't one for commitment, the friend said. It was the start of winter, I remember. I take up the big blue handset, wonder if I could ring someone. But the line is dead.

15

Back at the house, I check on Facebook. The internet is still slow. I call the 24-hour helpline. 'Hello! Thank you for contacting us. The 24-hour helpline is available 24 hours a day. However, all of our operators are unavailable at the moment. Please hold or press the hash key to leave a message.' Classical music starts. I put the phone on speaker. I open the kitchen window and go out the back. The music follows me into the day. I get a spade from the shed. I start digging up bits of the garden, looking for small stones. I like digging. I must try a bit of gardening sometime. There was no mass on gardening when I was growing up. Unless it was sowing potatoes.

I hoke up three stones and bring them in. I wash them at the sink and dry them with my Elvis apron. They're not sand pebbles, whatever they are. But they're good enough.

I put them in a triangle shape on the table as per the instructions. The classical music is still playing. 37 minutes on hold. It's not bad music. But I can't listen to it anymore. I press the hash key and leave a message.

I sit at the table. The instructions tell me to breathe deeply as I stare at my three sand pebbles. I wonder will them being garden rocks affect the spell somehow. I am then to recall the last time I saw my 'Heart's Desire'. That's not difficult. I only saw her the once, that day at the Texaco. This is to be done for twenty minutes. I set the timer on my phone. I sit, staring at the three stones. After three minutes, I go and get six chocolate digestive biscuits from the press.

I turn back on the timer and stare at the triangle as I eat. It seems to move. There must be something in them rocks. Weevils or beetles or some other tiny insects. I can't see any, but they could still be there. One of the stones has disappeared now. I get a bit unhinged. Then I smile with my freshly polished set of teeth. It's my blind spot.

After I've all the biscuits eaten, I settle better. I stare at the stones and imagine myself at the Texaco. She's over by the air compressor in the services area. Helmet on the seat beside her. She's pumping the front wheel. The strands of her black hair falling by the right side of her face, covering one eye, one cheek, half of her mouth. The leathers are silver in the sunlight. She looks at me as I get out of my car. I smile and walk toward the bike.

The phone is ringing. I get around three phone calls a year and one of them is in the middle of my spell. It's the phone company. 'Yes?' I answer it, fairly loud.

'Hello! This is Jessica. I am responding to your message. Are you having trouble with your SuperFast Broadband Service today?'

'I am.'

'Great to speak to you, sir. Can you tell me a little bit more about your experience?'

'The service is not SuperFast. It's SuperSlow.'

'Wonderful that you have identified that for us, sir. We want you to have the best internet service available. Let me see if I can make your SuperFast Broadband even faster. I see your package is modest. Perhaps you need an upgrade? Do you download large amounts of material or spend a lot of time browsing?'

'No.' Only since I saw her at the Texaco.

'Fantastic. I will just do some checks. Do you have the WPA key on your SuperFast Broadband Router?'

My head is still a bit confused by the spell. 'Have I the what on the what?'

'The unique nine-digit number on the back of your SuperFast Broadband Router. That is the service box attached to your phone line socket, sir.'

'Right. I'll get that for you now.'

'Fabulous, sir.'

I go out to the hall and find the number of the router. I give it to Jessica. 'Marvellous! Please hold the line, sir.'

The classical music starts up again. Teeth are a bit sore. Maybe I should go back to Noel. He could have missed something. Maybe my teeth aren't that great at all. I don't know anything about Noel's training. He could have done some SuperFast course for all I know. All the people who weren't in his surgery today can't be wrong.

I'll have to leave the spell until this Jessica woman is gone. I go back to the Facebook page. The internet is slow, but I eventually get to the message icon. I could send her a note. Might be a bit stalkery though. I'd prefer accidentally meeting her at the Texaco. I could send something like 'How are you?' Or maybe 'I was watching you the other day at the Texaco. Pumping your front wheel.' No. Definitely not. The law would be called. Maybe Noel would be on the jury. Then I'd be in trouble. I look at the blue button. I scroll away in case I press it by accident. 34 minutes pass. I am about to press the hash key when the music stops. The silence is good. 'Hello! This is Audrey! I am responding to your messages. Are you having trouble with your SuperFast Broadband Service today, sir?'

I take up the phone. 'I was talking to someone else. Jessica.'

'Great to speak to you, sir. Can you tell me a bit more about your experience?'

'The service is no good.'

'Wonderful that you have identified that for us, sir. We want you to have the best internet service available. Let me see if I can make your SuperFast Broadband even faster. I see your package is modest. Perhaps you need an upgrade? Do you download large amounts of material or spend a lot of time browsing?'

'No.'

'Fantastic. I will just do some checks. Do you have the WPA key on your SuperFast Broadband Router?'

'I'll go and get it.'

'Fabulous, sir.'

18

I put the phone on the table. I go out the back, into the shed. It takes a while, but I eventually find my guitar. Four strings left. I go back to the kitchen. 'Hello? Alice? Are you still here?'

'It's Audrey, sir. Marvellous to hear you again. Do you have the WPA key on your Superfast Broadband Router?'

'Is it WPA or WGA?'

'The key is WPA, sir.'

'Oh. WPA. I thought you said WGA. I'll go and get that so. Can you wait there on the line a minute?'

'Certainly sir. I will be right here.' I hear her tapping her pen.

I start playing my guitar. I play for a good while. It's nice to know there is someone listening to me playing. I don't know how well it sounds. I don't know any songs. I just strum away, carefree.

At the end of my performance, I give Audrey the barcode from the cornflakes box.

'Thank you, sir, but that number appears to be incorrect.'

'Oh. I'll check it again. It's out in the hall. Can you wait a few seconds?'

'Certainly, sir.' She's tapping the pen again.

In the shed, I pull a few things around. Eventually I find my Djembe Bongo drum.

I walked out of secondary school halfway through the Leaving Cert. I went travelling on a cargo ship to a port in Morocco. I got the drum off a street trader in Marakeesh. You play it with your palms. I bring it into the kitchen. I sit at the table by the triangle and start banging. The beat of the Bongo might help the spell along. It's good. I'm better with the Bongo than the guitar. But Audrey would be better able to tell than me.

I rang the Principal from a phone box on the roasting African street, funny coins piled high for the trunk call. I told him I was taking the farm over from my father as he was retiring. He didn't know the old man was only 44. Close enough to the finish as it turned out.

There's a nice beat from the Bongo. Palms on animal skins. Street trader told me the sound is the spiritual heartbeat of the dead animal, still going in the other world. The beat gets faster, it seems to want to hurry up in my hands. The rhythm is gone off by itself. I'd swear the stones were lifting up on the table.

I should have done the Leaving Cert. It would have been nice for them to see how I'd do. The Principal told me I was SuperSmart. Nothing to be done about that now. It was the year Grandmother died, I remember. All I came back with from Morocco was this Bongo Drum. I never did find out what was down in the Hold.

The microwave pings. Bacon and cabbage and potatoes. I got the YR sauce at the Texaco. It goes down well. She didn't turn up all day. She posted about the new chrome she got for the bike. She must have gone to another garage for it. She's posting more than usual. Spell must be working. I scroll down her page. Internet is a bit faster. Audrey fixed it. Upgraded my package.

I hover over the message icon. I could ask her something about the bike. I've nothing to lose. I could ask her to come to the cinema. I don't know much about films. Maybe we could take a ride somewhere. Maybe she has a spare helmet. She has the whole rig-out, leather jacket, trousers, special boots. The gloves. But it's a bit early for a message yet.

Dawn will be at 4.32am today, according to the internet forecast. It'll soon be Midsummer. Another time that is supposed to be mystical. You hardly need spells in this place.

I stare at the three stones. The birds are back tweeting in the Beeches. I start thinking about being parked outside the Texaco. I imagine watching her pump the front wheel by the air compressor in the services area. The helmet is on the seat. The strands of her black hair falling by the right side of her face, covering one eye, one cheek, half of her mouth. Her leathers are silver in the sunlight. She looks over at me. I get out of the car and smile. She smiles too. I start walking over. The birds are twittering outside. They're distracting but maybe it's part of the spell.

I imagine I can hear the beat of the Bongo, playing by itself in the shed. The stones seem to be moving again. I look out the window. I see the line of birds on the telephone wires down at the road. Maybe that's what keeps slowing down my internet. Maybe I didn't need an upgrade at all.

I go out the back, into the garden. The grass is cold on my bare feet. I walk past the clay squares where I found the stones. The birds are joining together. It's finally happening the way Grandmother said. The Dawn Chorus. The solid chirping coming up the little birds' lungs, through their tiny throats. The Bongo beat goes on in the background somehow. The noise seems like the colour of gold. Like the rising sun, blinding everywhere with light, all over the air. Harmony.

I park at 8 on the forecourt of the Texaco. The place is busy. People come and go. She is bound to come again eventually. She'll be at the services area, by the air compressor, and she'll fill the front wheel with air, the strands of her black hair falling by the right side of her face, covering one eye, one cheek, part of her mouth. She came once, she'll come again. There's always a second chance. The spell is working. Didn't I hear the Dawn Chorus this morning? If she doesn't come today, she'll come tomorrow. And if not tomorrow, surely by the end of the week. Or definitely by the end of the month. She has to come sometime. I can keep watch here. I haven't much on at the moment. Teeth are settled down again. I check them in the mirror. Shiny enough. I won't need to go back to Noel for a while. I'll just come here every day until she comes. Then I'll get out of my car and go over to her. I'll see if she wants any help. Ask her about the wheel. Or the chrome or the helmet. Or that I saw a glove here one day and thought it might be hers. I'll have to buy one for that. Maybe we could go for a ride. If she has a spare helmet. I'll buy one along with the glove and have them both ready in the boot. I'll definitely do that.

The bakery van pulls up with the delivery from the nightshift. I take off my seatbelt. I'll go in and get a cardboard cup of milky tea and a few jam and cream doughnuts while I wait.

# THE MOURNING

The lake is still. I park at the clearing they use for boat trailers. I kill the engine and pull the handbrake. I look back through the line of thin trees. I take off my seatbelt, take a deep breath, exhale. Silence. I wind the window and smell the water. This is safe.

I take my phone from my handbag. It has been buzzing all the way here. Conversations have continued in my absence in the work forum. Several new messages and notifications have come through. The daily demands for responses, decisions, uploads and downloads, password and registrations. I press the power button. The screen goes exquisitely blank. I look over the folders spread out on the passenger seat. I'd been trying to read them as I left town, speeding through blocks of text while I navigated roundabouts. There must be a law against that. I look in the rear-view mirror, turn it towards me. I run my hands through my hair, identify the shape of my skull. For a moment I imagine it in its naked state. I shiver and focus on my skin. I see what I imagine are fresh ageing signs, the collagen stretched and compressed one too many times and, overnight apparently, it has ultimately rested in the contours it has been twisted in around my bone shape for years. But those lines were there all the time, since early adulthood, their visibility to me and everyone else dependent on the light, my perspective, my mood and my application of what was once called 'paint'. But the sight of them still knocks me, ages me instantly. I look away, turn the mirror back to the rear window. I didn't really come here for a hyper dose of reality, just the opposite. I open the doors, my heels hit the tarmac, what I can see of it, it is mostly covered in black-brown dead leaves, damp and flat. Late Autumn. Hence the deserted shoreline. At the summer weekends here, there is never anywhere to park.

It's rarely hot enough for bathers, but tourists take the small boats out to fish or explore the shoreline. Some have picnics and even camp on the tiny islet at the centre, known as *Inis Marr*.

I walk around to the car boot. I pull the work files out of the way and get to the leather case. I take it up and walk to the line of trees, into the clearing by the water. There is no sand here, just grassless ground, millions of tiny flat round stones, a line of small boats. They are more like canoes, they have oars attached to the sides, one or sometimes two flat seats in the middle. They are held in place by ropes looped onto steel bars set in concrete. They are all full of water and floating leaves. I take a bucket hanging on a post, go to the side of one boat. My work suit gets spattered as I scoop out the water. It takes ages. I stop when there is just a small pool at the bottom. I hang the bucket back onto the post.

I should really have changed my clothes. I put the leather case under the seat. I pull the rope off the steel post. I bend, grip the end of the boat and push. The underside grinds on the stones. The boat shifts onto water as my face gets hot. I jump in. I take the oars and row as I perch myself on the seat.

The boat is silent as it moves out from the shoreline. The land begins to shrink. I start to feel free. The pull on my muscles feels good. I dig my heels underneath. I feel like I am getting somewhere, even though there is nowhere I particularly want to be. I pass through a large group of rushes, then I am out on the clear open water.

A few drops of drizzle fall. The sky is grey. I hadn't checked the forecast. The air is cool but not cold. I row for a few minutes with no attempt to direct myself. Then I stop. The boat drifts aimlessly. I can hear the gentle throbbing of water currents underneath. The drizzle has become constant. Yet the sky is brightening. Sharp sun streaks through. The make-up which I had carefully applied this morning is running down my face.

Raindrops roll along my back, lodging at my bra strap. My good suit jacket and skirt are getting soaked. The hair which I had blow-dried a few hours ago becomes flat and sticks to my neck. The drizzle fades. My clothes are sodden in the warm rays.

I toss off my heels under the seat. I take off my soaked jacket, unbutton my blouse. I shiver as I unhook the dripping bra. I slide off my skirt, tights, underwear in one slick movement. The seat is wet against my skin. I enjoy the risk of being seen. There are specks of houses now visible along the shoreline, but I am as much a dot to them. Even though I am unusual out here and they are not. Goosebumps run up my arm.

I turn and reach for the leather case. I put it on my knees. My fingers tremble as I open it. The shape and veneer of the violin, the horsehair bow, the green velvet inner cladding seem absurd amongst the water around me, leaves stuck to the inside of the boat, the dampness in the air. I put the end of the violin under my chin, its wood cold against my chest. I take up the bow, draw across the strings. The acoustics are odd out here, bouncing across the lake as I try to play. It is like I am too far out of tune, I can't get into it, the chords I play are so far from the carpeted wall of my music teacher's practice room, her civilised, encouraging tones echoing now in my mind from our weekly lesson.

There is a screech behind me. I swing around, expecting the worst, a boatload of office clients with cameras. But it's a flock of gulls flapping as they rise out of *Inis Marr*. I have drifted all the way to the centre of the lake.

The islet is only 200 metres in diameter. It is mostly covered with short palm trees. There is a clearing within. I can see the remains of tourist campfires, crushed beer cans and other plastics.

I row again, directing the boat to the stony edge. It grinds as it reaches it. I look at the pile of clothes in the boat. I place the violin and bow back into the case and clip it closed. I get up and climb out, feet onto the grassless ground.

I walk to the clearing, enjoying the dirt seeping up between my toes, the air wafting all around my exposed body. Dead leaves lift in the breeze, some stick to my legs.

I look around the clearing. The gulls squawk overhead, the noise echoing down the shoreline. *Inis Marr* was an ancient funeral island. The tradition involved wrapping corpses and gathering them at the mainland shoreline throughout the year. On a certain date between late autumn and deep winter, a day which was deemed to have mystical properties, the remains were canoed out here. Afterwards, the islet was set on fire, as locals prayed on the shore to complete the soul's journey. The ceremony which had to take place before the sun was high was known as 'The Mourning'.

I circle the clearing, the drizzle has faded altogether, the sun has become bright. I find a mound of earth to sit on. Leaves stick to my back. Rays come through the trees. The palms are waving in the morning breeze. I look out beyond the shore, where the lake widens out. I had always wanted to visit this patch of earth on the water, but I had never had the time until today.

I shiver, the air cold around me, raindrops spill into my eyes. My vision becomes glassy. I can smell decomposed bodies. Noises behind. I turn. There are many large men, wearing just white ragged bands around their waists. They all have long hair and beards. They drag cloth wrapped bodies off log boats onto the islet. The bodies pile up in the centre. The men ignore me, until one circles the pile of bodies and comes near. His eyes are blue, his hair is long, to his elbows. He smiles at me. I smell his musk. He opens his mouth as though to say something, but no words come. There is a barely audible grunt. The others continue to drag in more and more bodies. The man comes closer, his hand is on my shoulder. It is warm and heavy.

Now I feel his hands on my body, grasping my breasts, between my legs. I grip him and roar. I feel heat as he thrusts. I choke in ecstasy. There is smoke everywhere. I see flames all around us. The others have left. I push the man away. I get up and run out through black sooty clouds to the boat. I get in, row quickly. The log boats are all gone.

Twenty yards out, I see the man on the edge of the islet. He stands staring at me. The corpses are piled high around him, burning. I stop rowing. The sky is dull, the drizzle has started again. The fire surrounds the man.

I turn and take up the leather case. I clip it open. I take out the violin and bow. I place the end under my chin, the corner of the wood cold against my chest. I take up the bow. Then I stand in the boat and onto the seat. The boat rocks and then steadies.

Ferocious heat reaches me from the islet, burning my legs. I start to play. *Inis Marr* is a now huge pyramid of flames on the water. The sky is thick with black clouds. Fragments of smoking palms lift high, then float down to the water. Hundreds of them drift around the islet.

The skeleton stands on the edge, one arm raised as I play, the skull a clean dome, black holes where the blue eyes were. The soot fills the lake. Raindrops now teem, bouncing off the water amongst the floating flames. I draw the bow quicker, the tune carrying me away. The skeleton collapses in a pile.

I play on as the islet burns. I play better than ever in the carpeted practice room to the docile tones of my teacher. I play better than I have ever heard, in any place, on any day of my life, or in any other life, or any other time.

# JARGON WINE

We had always seen James Fahey as a bit of a 'box-head'. One of those hard-heelers that read at the pulpit every Sunday, washed and polished the car, cut the lawn in November, paid bills in advance, teetotal as far as anyone knew and he certainly didn't smoke. Pure bacon and cabbage. He was, we had always agreed when we gathered at holiday time at the home house, someone who had 'nothing to learn'. He'd taken early retirement from the county council, a handy number processing planning applications, gotten a fine pension and then, at the height of the Boom, set himself up as an estate agent. It sounded like he had finally started 'thinking outside the box', but really there was no risk for our James. He knew all the movers around town. It was only natural they would come straight to him if they were buying or selling. You would see him coming and going out of the poky little office he got for half nothing off a dying widow, his name in large writing across the top, the tweed jacket carefully buttoned, the red tie too neat around the collar, the same old maroon jumper, a pressed flannel over brown shoes. He'd probably never been ten miles outside the town.

But this morning I was going to bring him somewhere out of his comfort zone. We had a big problem at the top of a hill near the sea. I wouldn't have used him at all for this tricky assignment, but there was no one else we could risk getting involved at this stage. To be fair, there was no one else that would deal with us at this stage. When I rang him, I just said he'd have to be fairly flexible. I was doubting he'd play but he said he'd take a look. I could challenge him anyway, there was nothing to lose.

'Best put the belt on there,' James said, as he started the car outside the office. He drove up through the town and took the road for the sea. 'Do you have keys?'

28

'We won't need keys,' I said, fiddling with the belt.

'Bit out of my area, this.'

'No matter. As I was saying the last night, I'm not in a fierce hurry. We just need it on the market–,'

'Right. We can talk about that when we get up there and have a look. Is it this road?'

'No, keep going straight yet.'

As we drove, James got a couple of calls, but he kept them brief, rarely saying anything outside of 'Yes', 'Right' and 'Call into the office'.

'So what was he going to do with it?' he said to me eventually.

'What were any of us going doing?'

'And it didn't work out?'

'You know as well as me. You must have seen some falls. Did you know it was coming?'

He scratched his moustache. 'I always remember, fellas coming and going in the office. The high-viz jackets splattered in fresh cement, the up-turned Wellingtons, measuring tapes hung on the belt, business account chequebooks in the arse pocket.' I laughed at him saying 'arse'. 'Gentlemen on the edge. It was all going well for a while. Then one of those days…'. He looked at me for a second, his mouth tightly closed, the lips pushed out. 'I got…well, I got a bad smell.'

'This one up here. On the left.' We turned off the sea road and onto a one lane tarred route. It began to rise towards a large hill. It wasn't quite a mountain, there were bare fields with bony stock right to the summit.

As we drove higher, James said, 'This place must be almost in the sky.'

'Near enough. Now this left here.' I made him take a few more twists and turns. I enjoyed getting him confused.

'I don't know where I am now,' James said.

'Not far more.' We came onto the last boreen, the car jerked as it bridged potholes.

'This was to be the drive in?'

'That was the idea.'

We came to a galvanised gate and James stopped. 'Right at the top. He knew how to pick them.'

'That he did.' I got out and opened the gate.

James pulled up at the front of the site. 'It's a castle!' he said as he got out. The block walls were mostly built to six or seven courses. Along the front, the window frames were half-formed. Moss had started to creep up the bottom. The DPC flapped in the breeze which was stronger here. 'So this came to a standstill.'

'Good way of putting it.'

James got out and walked across the front. 'It's not quite at wall plate?'

'Some piers at the back. He had just ordered the hollocore before…'.

'Before…ah. Tragic.' James whispered, but loud enough I could hear. He took out his phone. 'I'll take a few shots.'

'The thing about the photos. Bank are happy with whatever is the current value, so–'

'Right. I'd say it's best to put it up on the website anyway.'

'You see, we don't want it looking too–'

'Don't worry. Plenty of weeds and potholes. Bit of that moss there. I'll keep away from the ocean view.'

'Good man. That'll do.'

James went in the doorway. I could hear the crisp leather footfall, the click of his phone. I walked back to his car, coins rattling in my pocket.

'Was it going to be a five bed?' he called from the other side.

'Six. One in the roof.'

I heard him circle the site, chippings underfoot, he came to the side. 'It would have been a fine place. Pity.'

'Pity about a lot of things.'

'What's that crater back there? Bit big for a sewage tank.'

'Swimming pool.'

'Ah-ha.' James nodded and slid the phone back into his jacket pocket. He took out a small notebook, leaned on the bonnet and scribbled a few lines. 'Just a few impressions. I'll tidy it up later.' He looked around and took a deep breath. 'Air is good. Few trees, view of the sea. It's nice.'

'I don't take any heed. Hie James,' I came around the car to him. My voice dropped even though there was no one around us for miles. 'We have our own special client for this. He'll go through you for the collars…I mean, you know, the bank–'

'I know, I know.'

'But there will be a bagging…with the cheque. You know, for us. Will that be alright?' I could hear the wind whistling up the partial chimney.

James nodded. 'Not a problem.' He closed the notebook. 'Now to find the way back.'

'I'll get you back alright. It's easier on the way down.'

'It always is.' He got into the car. I shut the gate behind him.

'I only really met him the one time,' James said, as we travelled back down the hill. 'Do you want to put the belt on again? Good man.'

'Yeap. This turn here,' I said, pulling around the belt.

'It was a good few years ago. In his supermarket. It was a Friday evening. I was getting a few things for the dinner. I like a bit of lamb with fresh vegetable after the week's work is done. Do you know what I mean?'

'I do.'

31

'There was an offer down at the meat counter and I'd got a nice piece of rack. I'd picked up a butternut squash and some mint sauce. I was just going up through the drinks aisle–'

'This one here James.'

'Ah yes, I remember this turn. As I was about halfway up the aisle, I passed a large shelf of Huzzar vodka, and just at the back I saw a different bottle. Even in the shadows, I knew the shape and colour of the glass straight away. It stood out.' He swung out of the junction. 'I don't know if you have heard of this south American wine, Jargon?'

'Yard On?'

'No, Jargon. The other language.'

It was funny to hear the accent he put on it. 'I drink beer. Don't know much about the grape water.'

'Now, I'm not a big connoisseur or anything, but I happen to particularly enjoy this Jargon wine and it is quite excellent with some lamb.' James adjusted his belt. 'It is a really sweet red. I'd have it occasionally at the weekend or on holidays abroad. So when I saw it, I was delighted.' He slowed near a road to the right.

'Straight on.'

'Thanks. And this Jargon, it's not sold everywhere. I suppose it's a special import. Usually, you'd have to go to one of the city wine shops. Or else order it on the computer.' On the straight stretch James picked up speed. He drove faster than I'd expected. 'So I grabbed the bottle and went directly to the checkout. I was lucky, the queue wasn't too bad when I got there. I had just paid for everything when he came up from one of the aisles. He stopped beside me and said, "Hello James". "Good evening, sir," I said.'

'This one here.'

'We're near the main road, are we?'

'Not far now.'

'Anyway, then he said, "I see you're a bit of a connoisseur with the red wine?" "Not really" I said, "But I do appreciate the Jargon." "I see," he said, "Wait a minute". Then he reached across me and took the bottle of Jargon away. He went down the aisle with it.'

'What was he at?'

'It was a mystery. We waited probably fifteen minutes. I didn't know what to do.' He glanced at me, the mouth tight again, the lips pushed out. 'It was hard on the check-out girl too. She was embarrassed, she just wanted to get on with her job. It was Friday evening, a big queue started behind us.'

'I suppose you thought you'd seen the last of him and the wine?'

'I guessed he was getting me a bigger bottle, a special edition, a vintage maybe. To be honest, I didn't think there were many around here that had even heard of Jargon wine, never mind buy and drink it.'

'Did he come back at all?

'I was just about to leave when he arrived up again. He was red in the face and he had nothing with him. He just looked at me. I'll admit I was staring back. I really didn't know what to say. Then he told the girl, "Refund James the price of that wine. A bottle of Jargon." That was it. He walked off down the aisle.'

'You must have been ripping.'

'Not really. I was excited when I saw the Jargon. It would have been perfect with my meal. But at the end I was more confused than angry.'

'This right here, James.' We turned onto the sea road. 'And you know the rest of the way.'

'I do.' He glanced at me once more as he changed gears. 'I'll tell you this. I never stood in that supermarket again.' We said no more as he drove back to his little office in the middle of the town.

On the edge he sits, he looks up to the sun, blinded, he hears the voices of workers in the front garden, the foreign tongue he has learned, he leans forward, feet giant in the blue water, he recalls a circus mirror, his forehead is damp, he shuffles, as though his legs are wings and he can take off, as though he can get away from the growing pressure in his chest, beyond the pool he looks at the burnt field, lines of vine trees, the cabbage-like leaves of the sweet red Jargon fluttering in the gentle breeze,  figures carrying baskets, beyond a silver lake down the end of the mountain, through the vines on the slope a child runs, pulling a toy tractor, the boy's skin is white, he needs protective cream, he wants to shout and warn him that he will get burnt, then he closes his eyes, the metallic thrashing noise he does not hear, he slides off the tiles into the warm purple clouds spreading through the water.

# SUNSHINE

If there is one job I hate, it is cutting the grass. I can't stop myself glancing out the window at the rotten blades. Karl's fault for putting the kitchen at the front of the house. Some modern idea he had. The postman looking in at you eating your cornflakes when he comes in the drive. So I'm stuck at the kitchen table looking out at the front lawn. I suppose I'm lucky I have grass to cut. It was looking for a while there that I wouldn't have as much as a flower box. I turn off the TV. Dr Kylie will be repeated. I toss the rest of the digestives in the bin, put the last of the sugary tea down the sink. That's right, B. Movement.

As I come into the yard, I see Lady Muck out on the road. Arms swinging, huge sunglasses glinting in the morning light. Fit-bit blinking on her wrist. Her head is tilted to the right, overlooking my front wall. She's checking Karl's carefully presented border of roses. The way she's walking, you would wonder how she ever sees what's in front of her. She must have a flawless report on every garden in the village – stop it, B. It'll do you no good.

I open the shed door. I climb around a stack of briquettes I had Seamus deliver. He has conveniently placed 8 bales in a way which ensures one can get in and out of the place with the maximum level of difficulty. I trip over an umbrella as I get around them and nearly go flying into a laundry trolley full of basketballs. I climb over Tracy's series of bicycles, from the Fisher Price plastic model to the latest, state-of-the art tourer Karl got her last Christmas. All of them equally redundant.

Karl's collection of *Kinks* vinyls stick out at the edge of a workbench which never saw much work. Karl had filled it with tools when we moved in and they're still all in the same

35

place. The only tool he ever used was the one in his trousers and he wasn't up to much even with that. I lose focus and take up the records. One thing we had in common was retro music, even more retro these days. I lean against one of the bikes and start flicking through the covers, the colours and emblems, attractive young men with morose expressions spark off the songs they used to sing in my mind, songs with stories in the oblique lines, the lights spinning over my head at a 60s theme night, vibrating bodies on a slippery wooden floor, a wet shift in the corner. Later me stripping and swinging off a disco ball, bouncers in penguin suits ordering me down, Karl's 'Oh, no!' face in the background.

Even back then there was some dick with a camcorder. I can still remember the way the amateur documentary-maker looked at me a few days later in the hotel staff house. His tongue out, salivating as he showed me the video of my disgraceful antics, offering to destroy the reel in return for a blow-job. I laughed into his face. I might, I said, if you had anything to blow, Junior. But with you, I'd just get fed up and bite. Show the film wherever you like, you rotten bastard, I told him. I laughed into his face. It turned up on YouTube twenty years later. It's got 238 views so far. I'm very proud of that.

The lawnmower is stuck underneath a pile of plastic hula-hoops. The remaining half of its gammy wheel is lodged under a bag of metal cogs that Karl was collecting from the dump for some fucking reason.

I should dump everything that's in this shed. I saw a documentary the last day about particle physics. If you looked at everything close enough, you would see the entire universe is made up of floating atoms. Sometimes, some of these atoms get stuck to other atoms. Some of Tracy's atoms are stuck to these hula-hoops. I pull one up. She is on the other side of the world, but her atoms are right here. Stuck to these hoops and these bikes. Must be why I never threw anything out. Except Karl. None of my atoms are stuck to him.

The three-and-a-half-wheel lawnmower bumps over the back yard. At the front I look to the sky. Blue. Sunshine. Not a cloud. Absolutely no sign of a good downpour of rain that would cancel this operation.

I pull the cord. The engine turns at least. It's not seized up. Not yet. Even though it's not been started since the back-end. I pull it again. It throbs limply. Story of my life.

Then I see the little red rubber button at the side of the engine. I remember I'm supposed to pump it before pulling the cord. 10-to-6 explained this to me the day I bought it, a few weeks after Karl left. I remember him asking me how everything was, if there was anything he could do. He was sorry for my troubles, he said, as though Karl had died, which unfortunately was not the case.

I can still see 10-to-6's head on his shoulder, chronically tilted to the right, as he adjusted the pull cord. He should have been called Quarter-to-6 really, or 15-to-6. Sensible chap. He runs that tool hire shop day after day, week after week, year after bloody year. 'It's a struggle, Bernice,' he said to me once, when I came to get the blades sharpened. He'd never extended the business. Not even during the Boom. Wise enough. Many of his flashy floored competitors have gone west since. Even the postman was installing an indoor swimming pool in those golden days.

10-to-6 has a nice smile. But he's not my type. I'm drawn to mad men. I've a collection of the fuckers. One of them even started calling me 'Madwoman' at school.

But 10-to-6 could be charming, in a 'You're my valued customer' kind of way. 'Pump it six times before you pull, won't you, Bernice?' he'd say. He'd be nodding as he spoke, as if to demonstrate the pumping action, his head always ending up back on the right shoulder. 'Keep the petrol clean and fresh, you won't have any problems.'

Karl had been using stale petrol. It had blown the engine in his father's machine. Of course, it was 10-to-6 who pointed this out, not Karl. 'I'm not surprised,' I said. 'He was gone stale enough himself.' 10-to-6 got embarrassed. His face went as red as the little red pump he'd his finger on just then.

I wonder does he know that's what everyone calls him? He must after all these years. I stand looking at the lawnmower, pondering. Imagine a whole town calling you by an affectionate nickname and you never knowing it. I guess people around the village still call me 'Madwoman'. I don't care. I'm proud of it, in fact. I could set up a blog called 'Madwoman's Meanderings' to pass the time. I was tasty with the pen at school. It could be popular. Or it could get me into trouble. I wouldn't mind a bit of trouble.

Lady Muck definitely doesn't know her nickname. That's because I'm the only one that calls her by it. And only in my Madwoman Mind. 'Madwoman's Mind: A Blog'. I like the sound of that.

Lady Muck must be halfway around the village by now. Fully updated on the state of every garden. The Lycra skin buttocks squelching with sweat. As if she's training for the poxy Olympics. Nothing affectionate about her nickname.

She'd better not catch me daydreaming on her way back. I pump the red button six times. It makes a squishy noise. I pull the cord as hard as I can. A limp throb and then nothing. Grrr! I shouldn't have to mow the grass at my age.

The only thing Karl cares about are his roses. He'll soon be here with his poxy set of forks and trowels and his pansy plant food, complaining about his palpitations. I'd love to get the clippers out and massacre the lot before he comes. Karl should cut the grass for me. But that wasn't part of the settlement. He has the drive and the rose border. I have the hungry grass. And this invalid lawnmower. And the shed and the house, I suppose. Fool of a judge really.

Karl was blathering on the last day about this special fertiliser he'd found on the internet. Roses are blooming since he started using it, he reckons. Panting with excitement, he was. It makes everything shoot up. We could have done with some of it in the bedroom when we were married. Once a season, if I was lucky. No wonder I went mad. I suppose he sprinkles it in his trousers for Cassandra. The Bollocks.

He must have dusted my grass too. Or the granules are blowing across. He thinks of no one but himself. I could just drive the mower right across the lawn to his border and mince up all those beautiful roses. I imagine his reaction. The mature version of the 'Oh, no!' face. I'd laugh as he cried.

I'd blame it on the local youth. The hoodied header element, spinning balls and knocking over gas cylinders outside Seamus' shop on Friday nights. I could set Karl up for a big row with their parents. But of course, there'd be no big row. He never gets into confrontation because he has to watch his dodgy heart apparently. But really Karl has no balls. It's probably why he's been obsessed all his life with the ones that shoot up the channel every Saturday night on the Lotto draw.

I remember 10-to-6 tilting the lawnmower to the right, to try and drive the petrol and make it easier to start. 'You might need to do that with this model, if you don't start it for a while, Bernice,' he said, as I tried not to notice the way the lawnmower and his head were aligning perfectly at the same angle.

I tilt the mower to the right. It's surprisingly heavy for a small machine. I wait for a few seconds, then let it rest again. I pull the cord. Nothing.

I wonder if there is in fact any petrol in it. I unscrew the lid of the tank. It's empty. Now I have to go hunting in the rotten shed for the jerrycan. I'm losing what little interest I had. I could just go back to the sofa in the kitchen. Turn on Dr Kylie. Another mug of sugary tea and a few more digestives. I might even light a fag. A smoke. The body warms to the idea. I've been good all morning. As good as I can be. Can't be good all the time, B. Can't be good most of the time, in truth.

This is my life nowadays. Getting excited about a cigarette, a mug of tea, a digestive biscuit and an agony uncle on the TV. This is what it has boiled down to after the childhood romance, kinky retro teenage discos, newlywed at 18, pregnancy, living with his parents, child's first day at school, communion, confirmation, Boom, fancy jewellery, big house, Crash, recession, washing dishes to pay for a second-hand clutch, house repossession threats, Karl set on fire, the police, a hospital, a counsellor, a lifetime supply of medication ('It's not you Bernice, it's your brain chemistry'), That Saturday Night, divorce court, mediation, now I stand here on a drive I no longer own, fighting with a half-dead, disabled lawnmower. My loin-fruit on the other side of the world. All I have of Tracy are the atoms stuck to her bicycle collection. I haven't heard from her in months. An Ex reappearing on a part-time basis to ignore me and adore his roses. The wedding ring is still stuck to my chubby third finger. Butter, vegetable oil, tractor grease, blowtorch, I've tried them all. I can't get it off, no matter what I do. Must be why the church chose that one for the ring.

I'm down to one fag a day anyway. I'm aiming for one a week by Christmas. If I'm still here at Christmas, which is not the plan. I eventually find the jerrycan in the shed under the Halloween decorations. I bring it inside and put it on the kitchen table by the carton of my orange juice-weed killer mixture. I light a cigarette, inhale the sweet fumes. I enjoy the risk of naked flame and flammable liquid. I'm a flammable person.

Out on the road, there's no sign of Lady Muck. The worst thing would be to accidentally fall into step with her. It seems safe enough. I start for the shop.

The forecourt is empty as usual. There's no one in the shop either. It's an old-style setup, with most of the goods safely behind the counter on tall shelves. The milk fridge at the door hums. I put the jerrycan on the counter. 'Hallo?' I call out. Seamus' collie looks up lazily from the front room. He never moves off that spot. Where is his fool of a master? I'd fill the petrol myself except I know Seamus has the pump turned off. He only ever turns it on when people are filling.

I go back outside. Seamus has a stack of briquettes by the door. Does he know winter is over? He hasn't a clue how to run a retail business. The place is still stuck in the 1950s. I'd have been a good shopkeeper.

I go around the back, down the little boreen to the store shed. I can see Seamus' bald head inside. He's loading yet more briquettes into a trolley. The man has all the seasons mixed up. 'Hello, Seamus,' I say at the door.

'Ah, Bernice. How are you?'

'Good. Nice day.'

'Lovely now. If it holds out.'

'I was just looking for some petrol.'

'Oh yes?'

'For the lawnmower.'

'The lawnmower? Are you going cutting grass?'

'Yes. With the sunshine. I thought I would.'

'Right. Is the pump off?'

I don't work here, Seamus. You do. 'I didn't try it.'

'I'm not sure if I turned it on this morning.'

'Will I try it?'

'Try it so, Bernice. I'll be down in a few minutes. I just need to bring down a few more trolleys of briquettes. You never know with this weather.'

'You never do, Seamus.'

I go back down the boreen to the forecourt. I open the jerrycan and stick the nozzle in. The pump is off. Of course, I knew that. Seamus only ever turns on the pump when he can watch from the counter. He waits until you go out to the pump before he turns it on. If you stand waiting at the counter for some reason, he'll just keep staring at you until you have to look away, so you can't see which of the million coloured switches it is. Then he immediately turns the pump off again when you've filled.

Seamus is terrified of losing money. He's never made any money. He's never lost any either. Bumpkin economics. But he'll never admit he has the pump turned off during the day on purpose. He wants people to think he is a good shopkeeper. But nobody thinks that. Nobody sane anyway. I certainly don't. He is not a good shopkeeper. He is probably the worst shopkeeper in the entire history of civilised shopkeeping.

I go back out to the store shed. Seamus is still loading the trolley with briquettes. 'The pump is off, Seamus.'

'Ah, blast. I must have forgotten. I'll turn it on so.' He follows me down the boreen to the shop, pushing the trolley. 'Fine morning.'

'That's why I'm cutting the grass.'

'The grass keeps growing.'

'You're not wrong there, Seamus.'

In the shop, his feet squeak on the vinyl tiles his mother put down forty years ago. 'So you're going mowing?'

'You got it, Seamus.'

Seamus squints at the rows of switches, as if he's never seen any of them before. He looks back at me, to force me to look away for the second he flicks the one for the pump. It's the only time I ever see him moving fast. Apart from once at a Foroige disco. We had a shift in the car park. He wasn't up to much. He didn't have a clue what to do with his tongue. Or anything else for that matter. The switch clicks as I look out the window. 'Fill away, Bernice.'

'I'll pay you while I'm here.'

'No, no. Fill up first.' Take care would I put two cents too much in the jerrycan and Seamus might lose out. Oh, I have him well decked. 'That'll do, Seamus.'

I go back out to the forecourt. I stick the nozzle in. The pump turns as I start filling. I can't remember how much the jerrycan takes.

The petrol spills out over the top. The smell rises. If I lit a fag now and dropped it, I'd light up like a Christmas tree. It'd be all over in a couple of minutes. Hot but fast. I'm a fast woman.

But it might not do the job either. I could be left in a nursing home in a nappy. Weed killer is the best way to go, so I believe. Sweeten it with orange juice, swallow it back, the wide rays of the smiling-faced sunshine across the carton the last thing I'll ever see. Said to be painless. A better option than scorched in flames anyway.

Halfway home I stop at the remains of the hut myself and Karl fashioned out of a collapsed tree in the ditch. There's a shallow pool of water under the trunk. We'd cut branches and weaved walls around the sides. When we had it all finished, Karl decided we should fit it out with supplies. It was the time of the Cold War in the 1980s. We watched the telly every night, waiting for news of the forthcoming nuclear war. Atom bombs were going to obliterate cities in a flash. Filling up bunkers was all the style then. I remember lightning striking one night, the whole sky went silver, I thought they'd dropped one of the nuclear missiles on us. I hid under the bed for hours.

We sneaked up to the shop one evening. Seamus' mother was asleep in the front room, Seamus in the corner, stuck in a book as usual. We took a wheelbarrow from the back yard and unscrewed the lock on the shed door with a screwdriver Karl had brought. We loaded up the wheelbarrow with sweets, minerals, bread, cheese, tinfoil, anything we could grab. I remember thinking the shed was like an Aladdin's cave, it was so full. Karl kept saying, 'Look at all they have, they won't miss a little barrow of stuff.'

A few days later, Mammy cut her finger chopping onions. I ran all the way to the hut and came back with a brand-new pack of band-aids. I was so excited to give them to her.

Seamus' mother wasn't too mad about it. The main thing was Seamus wasn't involved. The only thing they'd lost was the milk, which was gone off. It reminds me I have no milk.

Mammy thought the whole thing was funny. But the old man was raging. I'd disgraced the family, he said. He couldn't even go to the pub for weeks, he was so embarrassed. He said I'd be lucky if the priest allowed me to make my First Holy Communion.

I can still hear him shouting. One thing he was good for. No wonder Mammy took the ferry with me when I walked out of school at 16. The old man was left to argue with himself. What a ticket Mammy was! Waiting with me for the train on the platform in her leather mini-skirt and catskin boots! Us drinking vodka and tonics on board the old B+I line ferry in the Sea Bar. She bought all the drink that first week in London. There were nights we danced topless on the tables of the West End clubs till dawn. Mammy was more of a big sister than a mother really. She went so quick in the end. I can hardly think about it. I checked myself again this morning. That's one way I don't want to go. Hospitals, scans, consultants, waiting for treatment, slowly decaying into a pile of bones and withered skin covering, slurring and raving on steroids. I'm the same age now she was when she got it. No wonder I'm staring into ditches.

As I get back to the shop, I can hear music. It's coming from the kitchen. Seamus has *The Temptations* on full blast. I take a litre of milk from the fridge by the door. I knock on the counter. 'Hello? Seamus?'

I'm not leaving two euros on the counter. For one thing, I'll never get any change. For another, he'll say he never got it. Try and get paid twice, our Seamus.

'Hallo!' He'll never hear me over the music. I look at the piles of delivery boxes waiting to be unpacked. What is he doing in there, listening to old songs? Seamus hasn't a clue how to run a shop. All he's done so far today is bring up more briquettes that nobody will buy now winter is over. Seamus wasn't cut out for the retail business. Hard to know what he was cut out for. He had no interest in helping me and Karl with the hut. 'Are you going to jump into that book?' we'd often shout from the counter, Bubble King, chickatees and coco-cola bottles in our hands. He'd be stuck in that corner seat by the shelves in the front room.

Seamus was good at the spelling now I think of it. He could rhyme off anything the Master would ask him in sixth class. He'd be looking up at the ceiling as he answered, as if all the words were written up there. He seemed to give up in secondary school. He started failing everything. He grew a ponytail and a rat's arse moustache in third year. He had one of those clip-on earrings, a pair of doc martens and a black beret tilted to one side of his head. One time in the Art Room, me and the girls caught him shovelling his nose. On the way out, I said in front of the whole class, 'Seamus, did you have a good pick?' Everyone burst out laughing. He went beetroot. I can still see him as we walked away, our laughs echoing down the corridor. Later on, he wasn't at school a lot of the time.

Staring out the window the rest. He left in the middle of the Leaving Cert and went behind the counter in the shop. He's been there since.

None of it put me off him though. Hard to put me off anything with a pulse in those days. But when I cornered him at the Foroige disco, he was all picture and no sound. He didn't have a clue how to talk to women. There was none of the nice sensitive chat that guys with tanned skin, smooth accents and flowing shirts came out with on the US TV shows that we used to watch. All you got off Seamus was grunts and nods. Drilling my cheek like Woody the Woodpecker in the youth club yard. Big stain on his fly when I put my hand down.

'Seamus? Hallo?' I'm not standing around here all day. I've grass to cut.

I go around the counter. The front room is still the exact same. Brick fireplace, cushion-less, bony-arsed chairs at a small dining table, a wooden-cased Bush TV with a bulging grey glass screen and a column of giant penis-shaped knobs down the side. Beauty board halfway up the walls, for God's sake.

The door to the left leads into the kitchen. Seamus is stretched out on a chair by the table. He holds a can of Bulmers' cider at an angle in his left hand. His wellingtons are off, stood footless and slanted in the centre of the room. There's a mop and a bucket of steaming water by the sink. '...sunshine on a cloudy day...' blares from the Hi-Fi system on the counter. It's even got one of those Perspex covers for the turntable we used to think were so cool. 'Seamus?'

Seamus opens his eyes, casually looks over, as if a fly came into the room and not a customer. 'Hallo, Bernice.' His voice is a bit deeper. He smiles and says something else, about the can or the mop or his bloody Wellingtons, but I can't hear much over the music. 'Do you want more petrol?' I catch.

'No, no,' I'm shouting back. I hold up the milk. Seamus takes a gulp from the can. 'Can I pay you for this, Seamus?'

'What?'

'Pay you?'

I go across to the Hi-Fi and find the volume knob. 'Can I pay you for this milk?' I say, as the music fades.

'You can of course, Bernice.' Seamus gets up and follows me out to the shop, the woollen socks around his ankles padding the vinyl tiles. He grabs the two-euro coin and clings open the till. He hands me twenty cent change. 'Did you want a can, Bernice?'

He must be half-clipped already if he's giving away free drink. 'No, no. It's a bit early, Seamus. The sun is shining and I've grass to cut.'

'...I got sunshine...', Seamus says, kind of melodically. Is he actually singing? 'Sure you have the whole day. Feck the grass.'

'Feck the grass, right. I'll have a quick one so.'

We go back into the kitchen. Seamus unclips a can from the six pack on the table and hands it to me. 'Good luck,' he says and takes another swig. 'So you didn't get it cut yet?'

'Not yet.'

'You got distracted?'

'I had to get petrol. And then milk.'

'You had to get petrol. Ah yes. And then milk.' Seamus is still half good-looking. But he's still got nothing to say. There was talk he was afraid of his mother. His looks have faded now. Jaw softer. The hair on top long gone. Sprouts in the nose and ears. No one here to tell him to buy a feckin' tweezers.

My boots slide around on the tiles. The floor is thick with grease. The mop handle hangs limp over the sink. Seamus must have lost the will today. I know what that's like.

'There will be rain later,' Seamus is saying now.

'There will? Good,' I say. I can cancel the rotten mowing so. Get back to it some other day. The cider is lukewarm. It stings my throat, then warms my cheeks. I look over at Seamus, his eyes half-closing. 'Are you a big fan of the 60s music, Seamus?'

'Some of them. When they have a story to them. That one is about a man whose girl left him for another. Do you ever sing at all now? In the choir?'

'Nah.'

'You were good with the voice.'

I didn't really think you were listening, Seamus. 'Too much politics around the organ. I just left them to bicker away about the chorus amongst themselves.'

'I never thought you'd give up the singing. It was the main reason I went to Mass. To hear you sing,' Seamus says, as though out of breath. He pulls another can off the pack and pushes it toward me.

'I better be getting on with the grass. If there's rain promised.'

'Drink up. Feck the grass.'

The morning sun rises in the sky as we continue drinking. The shadows change in the kitchen. Not a sinner comes into the shop all morning. He'll surely close it up altogether soon at this rate. Seamus puts the needle back to the start and turns the Hi-Fi up. We get through the six pack.

Somehow, I think when he was getting up to get more cans, I find myself on his lap, searching for the lad I couldn't find decades before. He is bonier than he looks. He has his hands high in the air, as if I am holding a gun to his head.

'Bernice, please.' My hand is on his fly. There's no stain now and not much else going on either.

'Bernice, I need to–,' I pull off my top. I push my tits into his face, rock up on his groin. I get him out of the trousers, he's no longer as limp as the mop handle at least. I fit him into me, the collie whines from the front room.

'Bernice, I better be–,'

'You better be quiet, you fool!' I jerk up and down.

'Oh, my girl…,' Seamus sings with the music. I laugh loud into his ear.

Lady Muck is peering at me over the top of the hawthorn ditch. She is upside-down. 'Bernice? Is that you? Oh my God, are you alright?'

I open my eyes wider. Immediate dislike rises, followed by a booming headache and the feeling of being marinated in bog slime. I'm lying on a pool of marsh water in the remains of the hut. I must have wandered in after my sojourn with Seamus, during a mood of cider-fuelled melancholia. 'I'm perfectly fine, Deirdre. How are you?'

'Do you need an ambulance?'

'Don't be ridiculous.' I sit up. Water drips off my sleeves. 'Myself and Karl had a hut here when we were children, you know. I was just having a look around.'

'Did you fall?'

'Oh, no. No. I just got a little tired, that's all. I decided to have a rest.'

'But isn't that all…bog water?'

'Yes. But it's quite fresh.'

'You're sure you're alright?' She is shaping to leave. Thank God.

'I'm wonderful, Deirdre.' I cough. I must have swallowed some of the water when I lied down. Or it flowed into my gaping mouth as I snored. There's a funny taste coming from my throat. There could be a frog down there for all I know. 'I'm absolutely flying it. In tip-top form. You go and have a lovely day. You must be nearly finished your walk

49

by now? I think I saw you on the road earlier? It was at least three hours ago?'

'A circuit of the whole parish each morning! That's what my trainer has advised. The FitBit.' She flashes it at me. '15,000 footsteps already today! It's such a great motivational tool.'

'Good woman!'

When she's gone, I take my time getting up. Worst thing would be to end up alongside the crazy bitch. Music blares from the shop. The lyrics echo down the road, '…cause there's a place in the sun, where there's hope for everyone…'. Seamus is probably still stretched naked on the kitchen table. Good luck to anyone that goes there today looking for a tin of beans.

Karl's gold BMW is parked in the drive when I get back to the house. He is kneeling in the bed of roses. I can see his wavy hair flapping over the capstones. I straighten up and try to focus as I stop at the house. I still see four pillars instead of two and trip over the gate stop. I keep my head down as I straighten up and continue to the door. I stop at the lawnmower. I stare at it.

I forgot the fucking petrol. No sign of the milk either.

'Are you alright?' Karl says, carton of boutique plant food poised for pour.

'There is no petrol in this lawnmower.'

Karl puts the carton down. He gets up slowly, rubbing his chest. He places the new garden fork in his other hand into his new bucket, the shiny shop sticker glinting on the handle. He carefully takes off his garden gloves and places them by the bucket. 'I think I have a jerrycan in the car for emergencies.'

'This is an emergency.'

Karl comes across the lawn. He slickly slips out a key and clicks a button. The car beeps, the boot lid hums and smoothly lifts open.

Karl takes out a spotless green can and puts it by the lawnmower.

I fill the tank as he goes back to the roses. My head is raging now. I'd abandon this if he wasn't here. Put on Dr Kylie. Sleep the afternoon away. But I won't give to say, not with Karl in the garden. I pump the little red button six times. I pull the cord. A weak throb, then nothing. Grrr! The bastard is full of petrol. I've pumped it six times. What in Jesus is wrong now? Suddenly I am insanely thirsty. I feel like drinking from the jerrycan, do a couple of jobs on myself at once. I pull the cord again. Nothing. I roar at the lawnmower. My throat feels like it tears. Choky smoke from Seamus' kitchen as I rocked on his balls singing, 'I wish it would rain…'.

Karl looks over from the roses.

'Have you been drinking, Bernice?' This was one of the reasons I couldn't live with him in the end. He had no tact. He'd come out with the most simple-mindedly provocative questions.

'Mind your own shaggin' business.'

Inside, I take 4 Panadol tablets and put on the kettle. I sit at the table, trying to rub the blasted booming out of my head. I make my coffee and turn on the portable. Dr Kylie's talk show set fills the screen. The caption reads: 'Today: Relationships Gone Stale'.

Karl knocks.

'Come in.'

'Thank you.' He walks in and stands awkwardly in the middle of the room.

'Sit, will you? You're making me nervous.'

Dr Kylie is talking to a woman of my age. The caption switches to: 'Cherry, 47. Husband Willard, 48, walked out of twenty-year marriage for younger woman.' I turn it up.

'Tell me how the marriage started to sour, Cherry,' Dr Kylie says.

'I guess things really started to go wrong after our daughter grew up, Dr Kylie. We just didn't seem to have much in common anymore. Willard bought a motorbike and spent a lot of time away touring or else working in the garage. He became very distant. I couldn't get through to him. I felt very isolated in my home. And then to find that behind my back he'd met this other woman…you know it makes me so sad…'. Cherry dabs her dry cheekbones with a handkerchief embroidered 'Dr Kylie Listens'. Dr Kylie pats Cherry on the shoulder with his orange-sponge microphone.

We get a view of backstage, where a man in his late 40s and a young woman sit, holding hands. The caption reads: 'Cherry's ex-husband Willard and his new love, Petal, 21.' The crowd jeers as Willard kisses Petal on the cheek.

Karl has sat on the sofa. He taps his chest. 'Getting palpitations again,' he says.

'You were told not to exert yourself by the doctor.'

'A little light gardening is hardly exertion.'

'Do you want tea?' I shout over the audience booing in Dr Kylie's studio.

'That'd be great. I can make it myself.'

'No, no. I'll make it for you. If you're getting palpitations.' I say and turn down the TV.

'Roses are coming along nicely. The sunshine the last few days is great for them. I hope it lasts.'

'I hear there will be rain later.' I make the tea and bring it over to him. 'It's black, I'm afraid. I don't seem to have any milk.'

'That's fine.' Karl's lack of annoyance about this annoys me. 'Will the mower not start?'

'Is that not bleedin' obvious?'

Karl stares at the TV screen, where Cherry speaks to Dr Kylie. 'Tracy doesn't want to go back to Uni in September. She's heard about this Art degree at a special college in Hamburg.'

'But she's already deferred two years! Is this when she comes back from her six-month tour of Australia? Why did she have to go out there anyway?'

'It was some type of spiritual exercise her therapist told her to do. Anyway, she met one of the Hamburg course directors at a pilgrimage meeting in Bali. He told her she'd benefit hugely from the course. She possesses the ideal personality type.'

'Ten grand, I suppose.'

'I think the fee is seventeen thousand.'

'You keep filling up her bank account, she'll keep doing these aimless things.' My voice is lighter. The headache is fading. The tablets are making me happy. But I refuse to demonstrate any type of joy around Karl. 'Tell her she has to go back to college. It's psychology or nothing. That's what we all agreed the last time. She had her flippin' artistic period years ago.'

'I've tried talking to her, but–,'

'She won't listen to me. You're the one keeping the lights on. Next time she calls you for a draw, tell her you've ran out of money.'

'Ran out?'

'On the stock market.'

'B, look–,'

'Don't "B" me.'

'You seem a bit–,'

'I seem a bit what?' Headache is coming back. Useless tablets.

'Maybe you need a holiday?' Karl taps his chest again.

Dr Kylie is holding Cherry's hand as he speaks to her. I wish I could hear the words just then. An inset of the couple backstage appears. Some of the audience are on their feet, waving and pointing. 'Do you want to go somewhere? Dubai? Hong Kong? Somewhere you've never been before?'

'I don't want to go to shaggin' Hong Kong. I just want my lawnmower to start.'

'I can call a mechanic for you. I don't know why you don't let me buy you a ride-on.'

'I don't want a ride-on. That's my lawnmower and it's the only machine I am using. I bought it with my money from washing plates when you couldn't afford a nail clippers.'

'Bernice, it won't start, and it's only got three legs.'

'You think your wallet can solve everything.'

'No, I don't think that at all. I just imagined a week away would do you good. Out of your usual routine.'

'What routine? Sitting here all day, looking at the TV? I can't even do my few hours in the hotel anymore, because of your poxy wealth taxes.'

'You'd be working for basically nothing. There's great tours on offer at the moment for single travellers–,'

'You want to shuttle me off on a pensioners' cruise is that it? I'm 48, not 78.'

'I'm just trying to help, Bernice. Myself and Cassandra went to Beijing last month, it was an incredible exper–,'

'I don't want to hear about your girlfriend-stroke-daughter, thank you very much.'

'That's not nice, Bernice.'

'She's the same age as Tracy.'

'That's twenty-nine.'

'You're fifty-one.'

'What do you want from me?'

'To start the fucking lawnmower.'

Willard and Petal enter the studio. Cherry gets up and points at Petal. Willard points at Cherry and Dr Kylie. Dr

Kylie points at the audience. Two security men wearing black clothing and sunglasses emerge and stand at the edge of the studio, with muscular arms folded. Cherry launches herself at Petal, arms around Petal's neck, the crowd are on their feet, Willard puts his hands in the air, the security men drag the women away from each other. Dr Kylie nods, the orange-sponge microphone jutting into his chin.

I fit a socket wrench onto the engine plug of the lawnmower. It's tight as I try to turn it. I spray WD40 into the threads. Karl is back at the bed of roses, on his knees, untangling thorns from weeds. He's humming. Karl is not musical. The humming is just a lifeless drone. I should go back to the Sunday choir. I didn't know Seamus thought I had a good voice.

The plug turns in the threads. Maybe I'll leave the orange juice and weed killer mixture until after Mass on Sunday. I'll go to the church and give the parish one last blast. I imagine what I might sing. Who plays the organ down there nowadays? I start getting excited about it. I'll show them what they've been missing.

The plug comes out. I examine the thin strip of metal at the end. The electrical spark that travels through it creates an explosion which pushes the single piston forward, turning the crankshaft and then the blades. The lawnmower is powered by an internal combustion engine. It was invented by Alphonse Beau de Rochas. It's amazing what you can learn in a morning on Youtube. I rub the strip of metal with a piece of wire wool. I'd have been a good mechanic.

'Do you know what you are doing there, Bernice?'

'Shut up.' I screw back on the plug tight. I pump the red button six times. It makes that squishy sound. I pull the cord. The lawnmower bursts into life. For some reason. I'm reminded of the midwife emerging from between my legs, holding bloody Tracy. Karl sitting clueless in the corner, fidgeting with the farcical Marx Brothers scissors they'd given him for the umbilical cord. He couldn't even do that job right, spraying the midwife with blood as he awkwardly chopped. As the lawnmower ticks over, I feel like punching the air. But I refuse to allow Karl to see any joy. I push the throbbing machine into the centre of the lawn. I decide today to start at the centre and mow out in ever increasing circles. When Karl used to cut the grass here with his father's contraption, he would go up and down in strips, in the same boring way he did all his jobs around the place. He would cut it twice a week in the summer. After the Crash killed his career in finance, he hadn't much else for doing. He hadn't got around to saving for a rainy day. We were relying on hand-outs sent down from the Government. Bare subsistence for weekly groceries. I'd get a few hours washing dishes at the hotel in July and August. My wages paid for Santy, Tracy's birthday clothes. Anything else we needed in the house. He just sat in the kitchen every night, trying to figure out the magical six Lotto numbers of the 48. He researched the entire history of the draw, calculating what he called probabilities, patterns of certain numbers. Breathless at the telly every Saturday night, convinced one of his many formulas would eventually determine the final six.

He'd be sulking all night after. Sometimes he'd go with the phone to the bathroom and wank at porn. More action then I would get at the time.

I never bought a single ticket. The lottery was the biggest scam of all, I told him. Trying to pick the right horse in a race of fourteen million all running at the same speed, I read somewhere, probably in one of his trade magazines. It was too much money for a cheap thrill. It didn't matter what formula he used, his numbers would never come up. Until one night they did. He moved out two days later.

I was delighted he was gone. Free from his rules and regulations. Electricity rations, frozen food, blankets instead of oil heating, him grumbling about every single piece of clothing I'd get for Tracy, which I bought out of my wages. The night he hit the jackpot, it was me that won the lotto. I became a free woman. I don't need his rotten money. I could get half of it if I wanted. All I got was this house. We'd demolished the little thatched cottage that was here to build it during the Boom. The site was the only thing left of Karl's farm after his father had gambled away the rest.

The circles of the cut lawn get bigger. The smell of chopped grass rises with petrol. The fumes of fuel can make you high. I'm already happy enough on the Panadol mixed with the morning's cider interlude. On the last circle, I stop a few yards from Karl. He has his back to me. He is still humming, I can see his shoulders rocking. He pulls up weeds, flattens the clay with the trowel. As the piston bounces, I get an idea. I direct the lawnmower toward Karl. His roses are lined up in front of me.

Karl must have noticed something and turns around. 'What are you doing there, Bernice?'

I smile in the sunshine. I push the lawnmower off the grass and onto his roses. The first bush bends under the gammy wheel and into the spinning blades.

'Woah, Bernice, what, stop! Stop that!' Karl gets up.

The roses get minced, pink petals and green thorns fly out the chute.

'No, God, please!' The 'oh-no' expression is out now, bejaysus!

I push the lawnmower faster toward the wall, briars spinning as I tilt up the front.

'No!' Karl is blue in the face. I run the lawnmower onto him, the engine stutters as the blades get caught up in his flabby body, I laugh as he cries.

I watch Karl sleep. He is wrapped tightly in white blankets, his head sunk into the pillow. He is plugged into machines with blinking monitors. A woman with a file arrives. 'That number doesn't seem to be ringing, Mrs Watt?'

'Don't worry. I'll call Petal myself.'

'I understand he had been told not to exert himself?'

'It was just some light gardening.'

'It must be a huge shock for you.'

'I was just watching the TV and I heard roaring in the garden. He was cutting the grass with the lawnmower and he must have went into a fit. He went off course and his poor roses got destroyed.'

'Yes, he told the paramedics he was working away in the sunshine and he lost consciousness. I guess you know, Mrs Watt, that a stroke like this is a life-changing event. Karl will need a lot of recovery time. When he is discharged, he is going to require continuous personal assistance. A nursing home is often a respite solution in these cases, unless you are in a position to provide support?' the woman says, looking at the file.

'Of course I am. I'll take good care of him.' I tap the blankets around Karl's body warmly. I'd have been a good nurse.

# THE VIEWING

Ha-ha-ha-ha-ha-ha! I hear something! They are coming! They are! What will they think? What will they think of me? Oh, I can't wait! I just can't wait to see how it is all going to turn out! What fun! It's not half as bad as I thought. You would think it would be a lot worse than this, much worse. The way people talk about it! But really, it's not bad at all. Not bad at all. I'm delighted Jeremy did everything he was asked. Good boy. Everything completed as I detailed. Jeremy has had his demons. But he is not a bad boy. Not a bad boy at all. And now he won't mind me talking. I can keep talking as much as I want. I never get tired. Never. Not a bit of it. I don't feel anything bad now. All those aches and pains, sores and boils. Gone forever.

Never a twang. All gone for good. If I'd known all this, I wouldn't have been in the least worried! Not in the least! Uh-oh! What's that out there? There's more movement. There is! They're outside the inside now. I just know it. Oh-ho-ho-ho! What will they think? What will they think of me? But listen…listen! Ha-ha-ha! Of course, I don't listen. But now I know people are out there. I just know. I know it all now. I know the double entrance doors are opening. Now you see! See…ha-ha-ha! Of course, I don't see. Thanks to Father Wills. He wouldn't let me have that one. But I don't mind now. I just know.

They are all coming now. What will they think? What will they think of me? My plan. My way of doing things at the last. I was so afraid of leaving it all to Jeremy. He can be so jumpy with that…thing he has. I was afraid he wouldn't do what I wanted. He wouldn't follow my instructions. I was afraid Alice would get involved as she tends to do, silly girl, and ruin everything. Or Sidney, that slithering snake. But it has all worked out beautifully. And none of them are here. Not yet.

More footsteps. Entrance doors opening. They're here! They are! Now the room doors. Oh-ho-ho-ho! Voices. Someone is close. Wait…the brass knobs are turning! It's happening! It is! I am so happy! I'd be breathless if I could breathe! The metal is coming out of the wood. The lid comes off…the light comes in…

McGregor nods as we get to the entrance door. He gets out and adjusts his cap. 'Ron. Teresa. Good to see ye.'

'Never good to see you, Mr McGregor,' I say, making a joke before I think of it.

'Ronnie!' Teresa elbows me.

'Oh. Sorry. I just meant–'

'Not a bother, Ron. Jeremy is within. He was here early.'

'Jeremy is always very early, isn't he, Ronnie?'

We follow McGregor into the lobby outside the viewing room. 'He said there wouldn't be a lot of family,' McGregor says, his voice dropping to a whisper. 'I didn't think ye would want many empty chairs. So I just put out four. Isn't there another relation coming as well?'

'Yes, her first cousin, Sidney. He's been looking after Saoirse's house since she went into the home.'

'He must be in it eight years now, Ronnie?' Teresa says.

'Alice might be here for the service too.'

'Ronnie!' Teresa elbows me. 'Alice won't be here!' Teresa tuts and shakes her head. 'That's Jeremy's wife, Mr McGregor. But the marriage is dead now.'

McGregor takes his hat off and puts his hand on the Viewing Room door handle. 'So four chairs should be about right then.' He leads us inside.

Jeremy sits on the first chair. He is dressed in a black suit and tie. He taps his heels, his hands are clasped tightly on his lap. 'Hello there!' he says when he sees us, and jumps out of the chair, hurrying across to the doors leading to the toilet lobby.

We sit in the last two seats. 'Sweet Jesus!' Teresa blesses herself. She looks over to the coffin. But there is nothing in the centre of the room.

'Where's Saoirse?' I look down to the toilet lobby doors to Jeremy, who stares blankly back at me. I look around the Viewing Room. I eventually find the coffin, upright against the far wall. It is painted a glossy green. My sister stands within.

'It's what Maum wanted,' Jeremy says, as he examines one of the toilet door hinges. 'To be able to look people right in the eye at her funeral.' He nods at me and then presses one of the hinge screws. 'In case she wasn't…you know. Fully dead.' Jeremy smiles and goes out to the toilets.

'She wanted her eyes left open too,' McGregor says, in a whisper. 'We had awful trouble in the morg. But in the end Father Wills wouldn't allow it.'

'But what if it falls over?'

'Ronnie!' Teresa elbows me. 'Mr McGregor has taken care of all that, I'm sure.'

'Oh yes, it's very secure, Ron. Six-inch plug-and-screws bolted into the wall. She'll have left her mark when she goes, that's for sure. The only trouble we had when we got here was…well, you know we had to take her out. Fr Wills was here though. He okayed us to sit her on a chair while we were drilling. It was a quare sight. You'd think she was looking at us. I was glad when we got her back into the box.' McGregor folds and unfolds the cap in his hands. 'We lidded her again straight after, just in case.'

'In case of what?'

McGregor nods at an opened drill case in the corner.

'We'll have to whip her out again
when we're going.'

'What the blazes?' We turn around. Sidney stands at the lobby door. He stares at the coffin. He looks at us. 'Ah Jaysus, entirely! Where's the man himself?' A toilet flushes out the back. 'Ah, don't tell me. Counting the tiles in the jacks, I suppose. I'll go out to him.'

'I better open up for the public,' McGregor says. 'It's gone five.'

We sit alone with Saoirse in the Viewing Room. 'We should say a prayer.' We walk across to the coffin. Saoirse's eyes are shut tight. Her skin is surprisingly smooth for someone in their nineties. Her lips have been gummed into a smile by the mortician. She seems taller. She is dressed in a green cardigan, her wedding ring scratched and loose on her ring finger. Her hands are clasped around emerald rosary beads. We bless ourselves and stand silently for a few moments. I try not to look directly at her.

'I didn't think she was so patriotic,' I say, rubbing the glossy green on the lid.

'I think she just liked the colour, Ronnie.' Teresa elbows me. 'That's the colour of the house too.' She looks to the toilets. 'You should say something to that fellow, Ronnie.'

'What can I say?'

'Tell him to get out of your sister's house for one thing. You saw the state of it the day we were there, Ronnie. There must have been a hundred beer bottles in the front garden. Every room packed to the ceiling with papers and cartons. Three dogs roaming around the halls, foaming at the mouth. I'd say it's riddled with bugs from the dirt. And the way Saoirse and Michael used to keep it. It was like a show house. I wouldn't say there was a day she didn't hoover or polish. You should say it to him. Sidney knows what he is doing. He doesn't keep his house like that. He's devaluing Saoirse's estate. Remember, he already got two other places the same way, Ronnie. A big farm with one. Twelve years and he'll have squatter's rights. It's only a matter of time then before he makes a claim. That's all he's been doing since he left the army. And Jeremy isn't able for him with that …that bleddy thing he has. He won't take his tablets, Ronnie. Poor old Saoirse. If she could see it now. It's just as well she was offside these last few years.'

Jeremy and Sidney emerge laughing from the toilets. 'Isn't that the way of it, Jerry?' Sidney is saying, his arm around Jeremy's shoulder.

'It is, Uncle Sidney, oh, it certainly is,' Jeremy says, wiping his eyes, still laughing. 'It is indeed.'

Their smiles fade in the Viewing Room. Sidney coughs and walks over to the chairs. Jeremy follows, his face now serious, and sits in the first seat. He taps his heels. We return to our places. Jeremy jumps out of the chair and hurries across to a painting by the toilet doors.

McGregor comes in from the street. 'Are you expecting many, Jeremy? I'd say we should close at six, if that's okay. Father Wills will be here then for the prayers.'

Jeremy takes down the painting. 'You know your business better than me, Mr McGregor.' Jeremy tests the hook on the wall. 'But I don't believe there will be a large crowd.'

McGregor takes off his hat, folds and unfolds it in his hands. He walks across to the coffin and peers at the back.

'He's right there,' Sidney whispers to me. 'Most everyone that knew Saoirse is gone ahead of her. Michael the same. He'd be near a hundred-fold if he was still in it. And them being in England for years will keep numbers down too.' He looks at the coffin. 'Nice bit of engineering that. Bolted top and bottom, Jeremy was telling me. Plug-and-screw. Couldn't have it falling over.'

'But what's keeping Saoirse up?

'Ronnie!' Teresa elbows me.

'They didn't bolt her too?'

'Ronnie!'

'Lord knows how they'll fill those holes after,' Sidney says. 'Such an idea. I tell ye, people give death too much room. Ten years in Lebanon teaches ye about death. It has no place in life. But if you don't mind me saying, Ronnie, she being your sister and all, this trick doesn't surprise me. Herself and Michael came back from beyont with the madlad fashions from over there. They were years trying to keep that house like something out of one of them poshhoor magazines. Sure she was up shining brass knobs from six in the morning. Him out in that snooker table garden, measuring the grass blades.'

'It's not much of a snooker table garden now,' Teresa says.

'I like a nice garden,' I say.

'Gardens are artificial, Ron,' Sidney says. 'Nature isn't meant for that type of pruning.'

'But Sidney,' Teresa says. 'Saoirse's house. The garden. Those plants…they're weeds. They must be six foot tall? And the house. The way it is at the mom–'

'Ah, don't talk to me! I promised her I'd take care of it when she went into the home. Like them all she thought she was only going in for a few weeks. I told her I'd keep the thugs out. But do you have any idea how much it costs to keep a place like that? When you have to look after two other places as well as your own shack? Yer man over there, Jerry, the demented bastard, has all old Michael's money flattened with them crazy schemes he comes up with. A radio station last year, import-export the year before, a fish farm is the new idea, he says. I mean what the feckin' blazes is he at now?' Sidney nods across the space. I look over, Jeremy adjusts the painting. 'Ah Jaysus entirely! And now he's working his way through the mother's. I'm expected to be covering running costs. I wouldn't like to show ye the electricity bill. Them lawns would need a team of skins at it full-time.' Sidney shakes his head slowly as he watches Jeremy. 'He pays no heed. It's all left to me. You say you like a nice garden, Ron? If you ever get the notion for doing a bit, let me know.'

Jeremy nods at the rehung painting and comes back to his chair.

'Seems quiet,' McGregor says, now at the double doors.

'It's a shame really,' Jeremy says, tapping his shoes. 'Maum would have liked an audience.'

'Oh, here comes someone now.' McGregor fits back on his cap. He goes out to the street and speaks to the mourner. He takes off his cap and leads them into the lobby.

'The family are all in here,' McGregor points to us.

'I am family,' Alice says, coming around him. She looks over to the space where the coffin should be. She then scans the room as I did, finding Saoirse at the wall. Alice blesses herself. She turns to Jeremy. 'Jeremy. Sorry about your mother.'

'Hello, Love. Thank you for coming. How've you been?'

Alice walks by Jeremy and stops at Sidney. 'If you don't mind.'

'Hello, Mrs Boyle. Good of you to eventually join us.'

'I'm not Mrs Boyle anymore.'

'Oh. Sorry.'

'I think that is my chair you are in?'

'You'll have to go down the end, Mrs Boyle.' Sidney looks around. 'Ah. No more seats. You'd better see Mr McGregor. He's in charge. There might be a stool in the toilet.'

'I'm Saoirse's daughter-in-law. That's my chair.'

Sidney looks at the back of the chair theatrically. 'You know, I don't see your name on it, Mrs Boyle.'

'Just because a name isn't plastered all over something doesn't mean you can take it as yours. That's what the cuckoo does.'

Sidney smiles broadly. 'There's always eggs in the nest when the cuckoo comes, Mrs Boyle. This chair was empty.'

'You can sit here, Love.' Jeremy jumps out of the chair. 'Maum would prefer I stood anyway. She wanted me to look people in the eye as they came in.' Jeremy hurries across to the toilet doors. Alice sits beside Sidney on the first chair.

Two teenagers in hoodies stop outside and walk in the lobby to the entrance. They peer across at Saoirse. Jeremy folds up a corner of the floor mat. Teresa elbows me. 'I wish he would take his tablets, Ronnie,' she says, in a whisper.

Ha-ha-ha-ha-ha-ha! Quite the crowd in the end! Started off very slow, but I knew word would get around. My little idea! A popular one in the town! Michael would have enjoyed it. Standing room only at the finish. The punch-up was a bonus. Surprising what little Alice can do with a fist, and not a pick on her. I thought Sidney would be better trained in hand-to-hand combat after all those years soldiering! And Teresa pushing Ronnie's nose into the middle for a smack of knuckles! Poor old Mr McGregor and his silly hat! What fun! But Sidney the snake won't be free for long. I know all that now too. He will soon be the centre of attention here. Oh-ho-ho-ho-ho-ho! Well done to Jeremy. What a good boy as it turned out! What a life this is! I would clap my hands if they weren't clasped in beads!

# TABLE FOR ONE

I am having difficulty breathing. I stand back from the door. I can see the exotic blinking green sign overhead fill up the deepening crevices of my face in the reflection. The desperate scene I have just left still rings in my ears. I reach to try and find the safety of the wall. Is this death?

My lungs start working again. I look through the doorway to the comfortable mundanity of the stairs. The grey tiles, the generic, in-built floormat, the industrial ceiling light. I see the shape of the suit on the glass, the trousers crumpled, slid down to my hip bone, the jacket loose on the beery waistline long shrunk to a skeletal flatness. Even the breast pocket has a hole, the aged handkerchief caught in it. I look down at the faded pinstripes, dissolved around the knees.

I remember the day I'd bought it. I'd decided on a whim to tour the country in the monstrosity of a vehicle I had just drive out of a showroom. The clean rubber smell of the glass walled office, no dirty money changing hands, everything completed on a glue-scented application form, finalised by my scrawling signature formed with a green biro that ran out of ink halfway across the dotted line. The manager had laughed out loud. It made little difference, he'd said. An 'X' would have been sufficient.

We'd stopped somewhere in the south. Traditional musicians filled the main street with wild, carefree tunes, the sky was clear blue. Children carried giant golden wafer twin towers of multi-coloured ice cream, they could hardly get their little mouths around them, us hand-holdingly happy in the sparkling bloom of plump youth, flesh folded into rack fresh clothes.

I on the mobile, as Elaine fingered elegancies to decorate our new Palace-Home, I discussing highs and lows, fills and empties, profits and losses as I inspected my roll of ATM spat 'Caoga Punta' in the sleeve of my smooth Italian leather wallet, while weighing up the regular Solitaire game I played with the gold plastic in slim pockets to the front. I, the discerning gentleman suit customer, deep in conversation with Moxy, another candidate currently eyeing investments in unpronounceable but nevertheless spectacularly sophisticated sounding far flung plots of distant Asia, both he and I, painfully in retrospect, ignorant of the imminent bitter humiliation, still sunnily enjoying our thrones of glass power.

Now I stand still gasping, leaning against the aluminium doorframe, in the incessant invisible drizzle, water in ears, as I open the same wallet, now quite battered, mysterious white dots in the inner fabric bursting through, threads loosening, the windowed compartments still stuffed with those long obsolete cards I'd been too sick to dump. In the cash sleeve, I find a till receipt, an important phone number I had scribbled on a parking ticket but neglected to include the name, a bill folded up which had needed extinguishment some days earlier but was still sadly alive. Eventually I hack out a twenty euro note.

I get in through the doorway, grab the bannister, grateful for its solidity. I put one foot on the step and join it with the other. I scale the stairs in this sluggish way. I'd once sketched twenty storeys on a handkerchief over a steak and wine lunch with Moxy. Now the 1st floor seems an impossible summit.

I hear the oriental music play as I rise. It's soothing, accompanied by the cling and clack of cutlery, plates, footsteps, the phone ringing. My cheeks are blotchy, as I feel the warm restaurant air on my face at the entrance door.

'Table for one?' the waiter says, as he comes smartly around the service desk. He wears the name badge 'Tony' on his black waistcoat. He is fresh-faced, I feel aged beside him. I was in trouble the day Tony was born. I was in trouble the day I was born.

'Thank you.' Tony leads me past the service desk, by walnut chairs and tables, paintings of the orient hang on the dark red wallpaper, a line of thin strings with hundreds of tiny bells attached divide the space in two. The bells tingle as we get to a window seat.

'Glass of water?' Tony says. He brings me a jug with slices of orange floating around the ice cubes. He writes my order in his notebook, spring roll and lamb sizzle. Then he whips away the companion wine glass and cutlery, leaving just the placemat. As I stare at the empty chair across from me, there is a sharp twang of the bell at the service desk.

Tony attends to three silhouetted figures at the entrance. He leads them down by the swishing bells. They are dressed in black with stark white collars. I imagine it must be the aftermath of a themed stag night, the clothes change inevitably postponed or cancelled as had happened me and Moxy on one crazed escapade. I am just admiring the authenticity of the swinging golden crosses on the uniforms, when I recognise the bald head and shoulder-length grey locks of the parish priest. 'Ah, hello, Iolanthe!' Fr Goulding says, as they reach me.

'Hello Father. You're out on the town.'

'Yes, it's a special occasion. I'm settling in the new man. Please meet your recently appointed parish priest, Father Francis Franks. Fr Franks, this is Iolanthe Malone, a local businessman.'

Fr Franks has a shock of black hair and a plump but weak handshake. His strong aftershave lifts. 'Delighted to meet you, Mr Malone.'

'And Father Michael Moran here has come up from the seminary to make sure I go home quietly with him!'

Fr Moran laughs and waves, his withered face carefree. Fr Franks sits at the wall and begins inspecting the cutlery.

'Have you just arrived, Iolanthe?' Fr Goulding is saying now. 'Perhaps you would like to join us?' He gestures to the table.

'Oh no. Thank you. I wouldn't like to intrude.'

'You're more than welcome.' Fr Goulding and Fr Moran sit across from Fr Franks.

Tony has arrived with my spring roll. As I start to eat, I can hear the priests drift into conversation. 'But is that really necessary?' Fr Goulding says, his voice marginally raised over the mellow Asian music Tony has switched on. 'I've always had more than enough room there.'

'With respect, Peter, it's little more than a shed. It's a cowboy effort at best.'

'But I–'

'I intend…' Fr Franks lowers his voice, my mind jumps back to the black afternoon just hours before. The staring Sunday lunchers in the hotel, the smashed glass on the floor, the expression on Moxy's face. Sweat breaks out on my forehead as I try to think what to do now, I tap my feet, grip the edge of the table as if I will fall over, I want suddenly to roar, to jump out of the window, to get away from here, to get away from myself, but there is nowhere to go…

'I'll sit here so if you don't mind, Fathers.' I stand at the priests' table, the plate of half-eaten spring roll in my hand. They look up, Fr Goulding stopped in mid-sentence, Fr Moran holding a glass of wine, Fr Franks paused with a prawn cracker inches from his thick lips.

'Of course,' Fr Goulding says, gesturing to the empty seat by Fr Franks. Fr Franks stands. 'You can sit in by the wall, Mr Malone.'

The seat is warm from Fr Franks. I put the plate in front of me. I glance across at Fr Goulding and Fr Moran. It's like getting on a boat in the middle of the ocean. 'How are your two little daughters, Iolanthe?'

'They're gone to a football match today with their aunt, Father. I had a… work meeting earlier, so I couldn't go.'

'Ah, I thought I saw you in the hotel. Was that your old friend Maurice Quinlivan with you?'

'That was Mr Quinlivan, yes.' Fr Goulding must have seen me with Moxy early in the meeting, when everything was good-humoured, handshakes, smiles.

'Those girls will soon be making their communion,' Fr Goulding says. 'I was just telling Francis and Michael about your wife, Elaine, the Lord have mercy on her soul.' People usually go on to talk about how common the disease is, how unlucky Elaine was to get it, with her healthy lifestyle, all the voluntary charity work she did, a regular church goer, married to a successful local businessman.

Yet I was not confused. I knew how and why it had happened. Elaine was unlucky. But it wasn't the disease that killed her. It was me.

The priests do not take the usual route. 'I understand Elaine was a fine choir singer,' Fr Moran says.

'I'm no expert Father, but I was told that.' Few were the Sunday mornings I was in the church when she sang by the organ player in the gallery upstairs. I was either hungover, putting out a fire somewhere, or off on a jaunt with Moxy. I lose breath again as the years of people calling with unpaid bills spill out in front of me, Elaine left to explain my constant absence. And it got worse. One day, the VAT man came with a lorry and took all our furniture, the sofa, the big office desk I had, even the girls' bunk beds. 'Standard Liquidation Practice for Fiscal Corruption,' he had told Elaine, I could see him in high-viz vest at the top of the stairs by the girls' bedroom. I didn't want to hear how that was explained when they came home from playschool. The car we'd once toured the country in was towed away, the balance of the loan still payable to this day.  Eventually the house had to be given up too and we moved back to the derelict cottage of my grandmother. Elaine started working in the local mushroom houses just to keep up with weekly bills. Until one day she became ill.

I cough and take a glass of water, drink from it, it's cool and fresh. Tony arrives with his notebook. He nods at my new position without fuss and takes the priests' order.

'She certainly had a wonderful voice,' Fr Goulding says. 'I always thought if a colour could describe it, one would say she had the sound of gold. A blessing the parish got the benefit of it, if only for a few years.'

'She will sing in the Kingdom of Heaven for an eternity,' Fr Franks says, taking up another fistful of prawn crackers.

'Iolanthe refurbished the church for us. It must be over ten years ago now?'

'Must be, Father.' A team of ten working there in my name, but I never set foot on the job once.

'He won't tell you this, but he refused all payment, Fathers. Donated his time and men. A very generous gesture. And we weren't the only part of the community that benefited from his success. You helped many people, Iolanthe.'

'It was the good times, Father. It was the least I could do.'

'Are you a painter?' Fr Franks says.

'I was in General Construction.'

'Was?'

'I scaled down after the Recession. We…we had gotten a little too big. Overstretched.'

'It touched many souls,' Fr Moran says.

'It was a difficult time.'

'You couldn't have seen it coming, Iolanthe. Like many more. People got into large debt. They had no training for handling the kind of money that was around the country then.'

A flash comes of letters from finance companies wanting my bank account details, so they could lodge an average worker's annual salary into my account on low interest within 24 hours. All I had to do was sign my name. But I know the fault was mine. I could have dumped the letters. But I signed them and sent them back in the prepaid envelope.

'Part of God's plan,' Fr Franks says, chewing.

'It's all in the past now,' Fr Goulding says.

'I always think the past is a tutorial for the present,' Fr Moran says.

'The will of God is always present.'

'When you think of it, looking into the past is really a question of perspective. Your girls are very good children. You're clearly doing a great job there. That must be your focus now. Like the community is for us.'

Tony arrives with a trolley of food. The rattle reminds me of nights sitting in a hospital room, the machine by Elaine beeping as I typed abstract financial calculations on my phone or stared out at the porters passing by. 'Morning, the wagons,' Elain would say weakly when she'd wake up from the rattling trolleys, a joke about Roman history I didn't know. She still laughed.

'Have you moved in yet, Father?' I say to Fr Franks as Tony serves the meals.

'On Friday.'

'It's a fine house.'

'It needs some modification.' Fr Franks empties the bowl of veal satay on his plate. 'Tell me, did you build on that scullery at the back?'

'Oh no, that was long before Iolanthe's time,' Fr Goulding says. 'That was there when I came.'

'That is a relief. The methods used there were questionable, to say the least. I don't believe there are any foundations whatsoever. They built the whole thing on nothing but dirt.'

'I have to say it served me well.'

'It will be bulldozed away as soon as possible. Do you do that type of work now, Mr Malone?'

I had no plant anymore and few tools, but they could always be hired. I imagine putting back on a pair of steel-capped boots.

'I really don't see the need for that, Francis,' Fr Goulding says, spooning up pieces of lamb.

'It's also far too small,' Fr Franks says.

'You mean to build something?'

'Yes, I plan to construct a modern utility room. Twice the size of what is there now.'

'But Francis, there's no room for that. The trees at the back—'

'Of course, they will all be knocked.'

'What? You are cutting down the palm? But those are mature—'

'They not real palm, Peter. They're a weak strain of the species. Do you do tree surgery, Mr Malone?'

'Surgery? Sounds more like butchery to me. I planted those trees myself twenty years ago when I came to this parish. It would be a shame to cut them all down for the sake of a utility room. You remember, Iolanthe, it was yourself that dug the root-holes?'

I remember it all too well. On the hill of the Parochial House, happily working in my JCB. In those days, just after we got married, I did all the work myself. Out of the house and on the site by eight every morning, into my yellow cab. Flask of Bovril and ham sandwiches, overalls, the rustle of the high-viz. The comfortable rubber smell of the Wellingtons. The jingle and hum of talk radio to keep a structure to the day. A real appetite in the evening for Elaine's roasts and braised vegetables, in the large kitchen of the cottage. An hour of TV, us chatting late over mugs of tea, sleeping happy. Nothing went right after I started wearing a suit to work.

'I must have planted forty trees out there,' Fr Goulding is saying, his cheeks red. 'They've been twenty years maturing. And now you are going you chop them all down in a morning?'

'He giveth and He taketh away,' Fr Moran says, working through his vegetable satay. They continue to argue, but I am thinking of a large office, the oncologist explaining the spread of the disease to us, the funeral. The girls putting a wreath of 'Mammy' on Elaine's coffin.

'More water?' Tony is at the table, holding another jug of ice cubes and orange slices, his skin marble white next to Fr Franks' beetroot jaw.

I chew an After Eight by the window. Tony puts all the plates on the trolley. He wheels it up through the dining-room, by the walnut chairs and tables, the red wallpaper and the paintings of the Orient. The stringed bells tingle and swish, the phone rings at the service counter.

I sip the coffee. I rub my knuckles, now swelling. Moxy was quite drunk but his treatment of me in public was inexcusable. I would never see him again. I will meet Fr Franks in the back garden of the Parochial House on Tuesday. Maybe he won't need to cut down all the trees after I have assessed the site. I can see the priests walking along the street. Fr Moran gestures to Fr Franks beside him, Fr Moran follows, hands clasped behind his back. They all get into Fr Franks' new car. I watch the lights come on, then an indicator flashes. Fr Franks pulls out and drives up the street. Gradually the little red lights pixelate into tiny triangular dots in the blurred vision of my tears.

# THE HUNTER

The hands pointed skywards as the clock chimed. I pulled out the tray from the till, pocketed the float. It was light enough tonight. I took up the dishcloth and wiped the counter down. Joe Lohan and Mike Coady were all that was left. They sat together in the front bar.

'If you put tin foil around the steaks, it won't spill all over the place,' Mike was saying.

'Would they not be dosed with fat though?'

'Not at all, it puts a great crisp on it.'

'Put tin foil around it. Never thought of that.'

'And you won't be hacking at the tray the next morning as well.'

'And poxed with smoke when you're grilling sausages.'

'Poxed.'

'I always wanted to know how you'd do them venison.'

I went out to the lounge, picked up some empties, put the fireguard up. I shut the last of the windows and I was just checking the pool room when I heard the bang.

In the bar, Mike was on the floor. Joe had got off his stool, his hand on his head. 'He was just talking about grilling rashers.'

'He fell?'

'Went straight back.'

Mike's head was against the beauty board I once attached to a stone wall behind that was beyond repair.

'He don't look well.'

'He never looks well in fairness. Mike? Mike?'

'Puts a great crisp on it...,' Mike said.

'He'll be alright.'

'I'm telling ya, it's serious,' Joe said and wobbled his thighs. 'He was on about running out of some tablets a while back…'.

'Huh? Have you tablets, Mike?'

'The pocket…'. I checked his jacket. There was nothing there. Mike's eyes were closed. He groaned. 'He's gone off again.'

'You better call this number,' Joe said, and took out a card.

'"Dr Luke Ramsay". This his doctor?'

'Ring him man, Miking needs seeing ta!'

I took out my phone as Joe whimpered at the counter. I could hear the strains of Mike's breath.

'Oh Miking, what'll we do!'

'Yes?' the voice came on the phone.

'Is this Dr Ramsay?'

'Yes.'

'We need a doctor. There's a man here after collapsing off his stool.'

I gave Ramsay the directions. Myself and Joe pulled Mike up onto one of the wall benches.

'Should we be moving him but? I saw on telly–,' Joe said, during the awkward operation.

'It's not a car crash. I don't think he'd break many bones coming off a barstool.'

'With them stones slabs you have you wouldn't know.'

'What are the tabs for?'

'Could be the heart.'

We sat in the bar listening to Mike muttering and gasping for half an hour about tablets and rashers until the door hinges squealed and Ramsay came in. He poked the stone with a walnut walking stick, carried a small black bag and took into a prolonged bout of coughing as he entered.

'Gentleman,' Ramsay said eventually. 'Not an easy place to find.'

Mike groaned. Ramsay went across to him. After a minute, he checked the wrist. 'Well, that's not a good start.'

'What's that, doc?' Joe said.

'There's no pulse. Ho–hum. Was he taking any tablets?'

'He ran out a few days ago. He meant to get some.'

'Pity he didn't.' Ramsay turned to me. 'You better call the priest.'

'That bad, is it?'

'Only one that can do anything for him now.'

We stood back from the remains, as though Mike was gone radioactive.

'Do you want a tea?' I said then to Ramsay.

'Actually, I have to go straight to another call,' Ramsay said. He coughed as he zipped up his bag. He reached for his walking stick. 'You will tell the relatives?'

'There's no relatives,' Joe said. He'd sat back on the bar stool, swirled the last mouthful of stout in his glass. Mike's pint was gone flat.

'Ah. Well, I better be on my way, gentlemen,' Ramsay said. 'So,' he looked at Joe and then me. He nodded at the phone on the counter. 'You were the caller, I believe?'

I looked at Mike, eyes shut, hands clasped together on his stomach. I turned to Joe, he sank the last of the pint.

'Joe–'.

'Bad business, bad business. I'm off.' Joe started for the door.

'Hang on Joe, this is your doctor.'

'Not my man. Someone gave me that card. I don't know where it came from. Might not be mine at all. This jacket is out of the charity shop. Good luck!' Joe opened the door, the hinges squealed, he went outside.

'So I really should be off,' Ramsay said to me. 'It's just fifty.'

'But…'. My hands reached the light float in my pocket. I looked at Mike, then went to the door before it shut.

'Joe! Get back here! This is your doctor!'


It took me a long time to find Ramsay's place. It was in the centre of a copse wood, overlooking a narrow stretch of the lake. I drove through an ancient stone arch and I came to a small wooden chalet, painted white. A battered Fiat was parked beside a small homemade dog kennel.

As I got out, I heard a tapping noise. I looked at one of the windows. Ramsay, still in the navy suit and tie he'd worn in the bar, waved at me, a sealant gun in one hand.

'Ah hello…,' I heard the muffled voice. 'Could you help me out?' he pointed across to the trees on the other side of the Fiat. There were six clear plastic tubes hanging off low branches. I looked back at Ramsay and now he pointed to the kennel, there was a bag of grain inside.

I nodded, took the bag and began filling the tubes. Kernels blew off on the breeze as I poured. I heard the front door open. 'That's a great relief to me.'

I filled the last one and put the bag back in the kennel.

'Come inside, please,' Ramsay was saying now. The chalet had a couple of doors at the end of one large room with a tiny kitchenette in the corner. There was a window over the sink and a large noticeboard on a short wall next to what I guessed was a toilet. Door keys hung on the board, the hooks were numbered up to 37. Ramsay put the sealant gun on the window sill, went to the sink and filled a pot of water.

'Take a seat,' he said, and lit the gas plate on the cooker.

'I'll just have a leak.'

Ramsay pointed at the toilet door. The cubicle was tiny. There was a plastic raised seat extension placed on the bowl. 'Be careful,' I heard him. 'But please, you mustn't move the seat. It is perfectly aligned.'

'Damn damp air always jogs the kidneys,' Ramsay said, when I came out. Beside a table covered in books and newspapers, there were three hard chairs. I sat on one and looked at a line of moose heads mounted along the back wall.

Ramsay stood watching the pot. 'I'm not able to reach those tubes these days. But I like to feed them. I'm very fond of their noise since Blue bought it.'

'Blue?'

'My Alsatian.' Steam began to rise from the pot. 'Liver cancer. Sharp and swift in his case. Mercy. Not rotting away here like me. 84 last January.'

I nodded at the walking stick against the table. 'You still work?'

'Have to.' Ramsay burst into a bout of coughing and then filled two fisherman's enamel mugs with water and teabags. 'I have no milk. There's cream.'

'Cream? In tea?'

'It's how the Queen takes it.'

'Black is fine.'

Ramsay carried the mugs over, pipe in his mouth. I took out the fifty and put it on the table as he sat across from me.

'Messy business,' Ramsay said, taking the pipe out again. 'No more bar calls for Ramsay. Past the parcel. Every time.'

'Blathering about rashers one minute and then…'.

'They all have their own crippled way of walking.' Ramsay lit the pipe, the tobacco smelt like an exotic wood.

'Sorry about the delay, my takings are…'.

'Don't say another word. I quite understand. No one gets rich from those...'. There were shuffling noises in the ceiling. Ramsay saw me looking up as he put the pipe away.

'Pine martens,' he said.

'Birds?'

'They're like weasels. They live up there.'

'They live in the roof?'

'Peculiar creatures.'

'What do they do up there?'

'They come and go. Do you want to see them? There's a ladder in the bedroom.'

'I'll leave it today.' I nodded at the silicon. 'Were you doing some DIY?'

'I came back here Wednesday. Two old gentlemen at my window. One with a fishing rod. Trying to unhook the keys.' Ramsay waved at the noticeboard. 'My houses in town.'

I reached for the mug on the table.

'Even had the damn gall to hang their jackets on my gatepost as they went to work. Blue used to keep this nonsense at bay. Now I'm wide open. I blocked the gate, called the law. Three hours later they arrived.'

The black tea was sour in my throat. There was chirping outside. The birds were at the tubes. I saw one trying to get its beak in further then the hole would allow.

'The cleverness of the bird,' Ramsay said. 'The nests they build. The way they emigrate. The way they can fly. In perfect formation. And the tiny brains they were blessed with.'

'Never thought of that.'

'My field originally. Neuroscience.'

'Brain surgeon?'

'Amazing thing the brain. When you look at it in a bowl. Just tissue and blood vessels. Where the mind is…that's where all the disgusting foolery comes from. I never blame the rest of it. Involuntary.'

'Did they arrest the two old boyos?'

'Young men. Teenagers, actually.'

'You said they were old?'

'No.' Ramsay inspected his pipe. 'No, I didn't say that. Policemen simply told them to be on their way. Not to do it again.'

'They'll hardly come back here.'

'Unlikely. I have a bolt action Winchester under the bed if any of them do.' Ramsay drew on the pipe, the little pot glowed red.

'Were you a hunter?'

Ramsay glanced back at the moose heads. 'Near the Alps. Winters in the late 70s. Cold dry air. Blood on the snow. Beautiful.' Puffs of smoke lifted around him. 'Double-shoulder shots. Round enters the blade one side, drives on to the far end. The whole body flexes and cracks its own spine. Anatomical masterpiece.' He gazed at the pipe now in his hand. 'Not a meat-eater's strategy but I was in it for the kill.' He sipped the mug. 'Airbussed them home. Some call taxidermy morbid. But to me, it's respect. Memory.'

I stood. 'More tea?'

'No. I best be going.'

'Sure you don't want to take a look upstairs?'

'No thanks, not today.'

I closed the door and walked past the birds, still nibbling on the grain. There was a small mound of stones beside one tree, with a dog collar nailed to a little stick at the end. One of the stones was painted a light blue.

There was a tapping on the window. I turned around, Ramsay stood behind the glass, pipe in mouth, sealant gun back in his hand. He waved. I nodded and then looked beyond the trees to the two large gateposts by the lake. As I opened the jeep door, I could still hear the pine martens, I could imagine their little feet endlessly scuttling over and back Ramsay's ceiling.

# THE WALKER

I stop walking on the hard shoulder. There is a light flashing in the distance. It's different from the yellow glow of the streetlights. A silver torch beam from the bog, over the sparkles of tarmac, through the hue of the blue moon. Now it lights up the canvas of a small tent. There is someone inside. It's a female. I know by the shape of the shoulders. I better be careful.

I always leave the city when the buses stop running. The clubs are starting, there's queues of youngsters lined up, perfumed, heels tapping, phones blinking, excitement of the night to come. I hit for the ring road, past the 24-hour service station. Around the big roundabout and onto the east route. I walk fast. I go if it's dry, if it rains, if it snows. I take what comes. I go no matter what. I probably shouldn't walk on the dual carriageway. But I live with risk.

There isn't much notice taken out here after dark. The night has its own laws. I could go by the old road. There's a lot of hills that way. But I'd get over them. Or I could go cross-country. I have done. Squelching across the bog, trawling through streams, climbing over fences. The world slows you down. It's never in a hurry. Nature is always on time.

But my old boots are leaking this last while. You can get no wear out of anything these days. I only have them a few years. I can feel the damp coming in already. Even though the shape of this road rolls down from the centre, there is still a film of dampness across it. I sense it coming in my woollen socks. Around the toes. The reeds and marsh are out for now. I'm afraid I'll have to get new boots for the winter. Then I might take on the cross-country. But the motorway is the most direct. As-the-crow-flies.

They knew what they were doing when they set it out. I know all about road-making. I did an exam on it. I studied the production of road coverings, bridge-building, urban and rural planning, infrastructural strategies and policies, waterways, dams. The route was well planned. On certain parts of the road, you can see the track of it for miles by the lights each side. You can see things better in the darkness of the night.

It's hard to get silence in the world these days. I've tried lots of places. The church. The last morning, I found a couple of parishioners by the devotion candles. Chatting as I knelt and prayed. Down the library. A row broke out one day over an unpaid fine while I was looking for a history book. You can't even walk along the canal in the daytime, without whooping children rattling crisp bags, beeping mobile phones. People racing everywhere. Round in circles.

I'd only be about during the night if I could. Sounds that were hidden all day come alive at night. The rustling on leaves, doors banging, bins emptying, dogs barking. You couldn't hear them things during the day. Not with all that goes on. But I wouldn't be the first to throw light on that.

No cars have passed for a while. Awful waste of a good road really. Lying dormant here for hours. It's funny to be walking slow on a surface designed for great speed. The road tries to hurry you. But I'll not be hurried.

It's like you are in slow motion. The big white and yellow lines, the flat bitumen skin, the crash barrier of two aluminium channels running all the way. The massive green and blue signs. The smaller yellow ones with bars showing how many hundred metres before the next turn-off. Billboards at the slip roads. Designed for people zooming by. You get a glimpse of a woman using a shiny lawnmower or a man filling a sleek washing-machine. Happy people that have something the drivers of the cars should buy. You see it. You want to buy it. But I'm looking at these pictures for a long time as I walk. When you come up close to the giant board, you see them better. You see it as a flat sheet of colours and shapes. If you look really close, you can see it's just lines of coloured full stops.

The hostel lobby clock put temperatures at between 4 and 5 Celsius tonight. The autumn is dying. The leaves won't be rustling for much longer. Except in the Copper Beeches. And the evergreens. I'm an evergreen. I don't lose my leaves in the winter. I don't hibernate. I keep going all year round.

I've decided I'll move out of the hostel as soon as I can. I'm in one of six bunk beds in a room. The people change every night. But even so, they're the same. Rattling plastic bags. Fiddling with zips. Blowing hairdryers. Flashing phones. I get cold with those noises. Scratching at you. Great silence out here. I was always fond of the night.

I didn't want to go to bed at all when I was a boy. The old man would tell me it was time. I'd spell 'N-O'. He would spell 'Y-E-S'. But I couldn't spell 'Just another half-hour?' The old man was good at spelling.

There's always hassle in the hostel. One night in there I thought I heard the cuckoo. I never heard one, even though I lived in the country until I grew up. I was awful excited. To hear the cuckoo for the first time, and in the city. I jumped down off the bunk, the man sleeping below groaned, rattling the wooden bead necklace he wore. I ran to the window. It was like waking up Christmas morning, running to the bottom of the tree to see what the man in red had brought.

I looked across the roofs. There were owls hooting by this time as well. Another first. I couldn't believe it. But I couldn't see any birds. I thought they must have all their nests under the eaves. Then I saw a square blue light reflected in the glass. The man with the wooden necklace was sitting up in the bed. He had his phone out. He turned off his alarm. The owls and cuckoos stopped.

I don't need to find anywhere else when I leave. I'll firm up for the winter. It's surprising what the body can attune itself to. Surprising what the skeletal structure, the muscular tissue, the organs can withstand. It's a durable design. Almost limitless. You'd be minted if you owned the patent.

I've tested it well already. I was able to hop sixteen foot when I was sixteen years. The long jump at the village sports day. The sports field was green grassed. White fence posts and blue ropes marked out the running track. Crease suit lines ran in huge decreasing circles for the laps and relays. Wooden swing boats rose high into the blue sky. Children laughed. A man in a suit walked around speaking into an orange spongy microphone with a short piece of wire that wasn't connected to anything. His voice came out of two blue loudspeakers attached to the top of a telegraph pole. I always wanted a go on that microphone. You could hear him speak all over the village, giving the results of the under-10s three-legged race. But I didn't mind the noise then. I always loved the night though.

The Schoolmaster in the village shook my hand and gave me the winner's trophy. It had a small golden statue of a man in sports gear. The Master's name was Joe. But he wasn't my teacher anymore by then. When he gave me the trophy, I could have said 'Thanks, Joe', if I wanted. But I didn't. I said 'Thanks, sir.' The Master told me I should take sport more seriously. I had a real talent, he said. I could jump very high as well. And I could run fast. I looked at the trophy as he talked, my fingers on the marble base, the little golden plate glued on, inscribed with the year and the word: 'Winner'. The man in the suit said my name into the orange microphone. It came out the two blue loudspeakers on the telegraph pole for everyone in the village to hear. They took my photograph. Everyone clapped for a long time.

But I didn't take sport more seriously. I went learning about the roads instead. The old man told me it was more secure. One of the arms broke off the trophy figure a while later. I never did any sport again. That was fifty years ago.

86

I'm still fit enough. I walk most of the day as well. It's surprising what the body can train itself to do. Imagine all the miles I could walk over another twenty years if I keep in good shape. No one should ever be in any hurry. Nature is always on time.

I moved out of the flat in the city a month ago. The crowd I was living with were fairly lively. 'Sticky People' the landlord called them. He didn't mean me. If they were all like me, he'd be elected, he said. But they're not all like me. That was the problem. He was getting rid of the lot of them.

The buck from down the country that called a kettle a 'kittle'. The foreigner that was trying to learn English from him. The father of three whose family lived in a different continent. There were a few women there too. I didn't know much about any of them. They're all sticky people, the landlord said. He wanted to clean the place up and get in a family. Every landlord wants a family.

I didn't mind. I was glad to be getting out of there. I took a top bunk in the hostel. But I'll be getting away from there soon enough too. Sticky people in it and all. Out here on the road, there's none of that. It's all left to you. Freedom.

I looked at a few places last week. But I didn't like the terrain. I'll firm up for the winter instead. I'll wear two trousers and two shirts if temperatures go below zero. My woollen cap. Thick socks and gloves. I'm fit for anything. I'll sleep behind the crash barrier on the motorway. It's surprising what the body can attune itself to if the mind is right. The mind is a powerful tool. The old man told me that once.

I'm getting very close to the torch beam in the bog. I can see the tent better now. It definitely wasn't there last night. Someone sleeping by the motorway. Moved in under cover of the day. Someone with my idea. I can see the woman inside. I can make out the jawline. The shape of the hair. It would be funny if I hopped the barrier and called in to her. Tell her I pass this way every night. Maybe she could do with something brought from the city 24-hour next time I'm passing. A carton of milk. Or a pound of sausages. Or a bottle of 7up. But I don't talk much to women. Never did. It's hard to know what to say to them. They're not straightforward. The old man told me that once. They can be sticky. The night is not sticky. The night is straightforward.

But it would be funny if I told her I was going to be her neighbour. That I'd the same idea. Except without a tent. She'd probably call the law. Say I was some weirdo. There'd be a court visit. A cell at the finish. That'd be the end of the freedom. I value my liberty. I pass by her tent and keep going. Good luck to her. She'll have to do her own shopping.

I turn onto the slip road after the last yellow sign. I walk up a little hill to the bridge overhead. I walk across, looking over and back at the carriageway, streetlights stretching out into the dark. I can see the tent in the bog. A small triangle of canvas-shaded light. I go by a little roundabout. Then I come into the suburbs. Streetlights shine torch beam silver here instead of the motorway yellow. Security alarms flash in industrial estates. Lines of trucks parked up all night. Awful waste really. The night is a neglected space.

Near the town centre, I cross an old bridge. I stop in the middle, go to the wall, look into the canal. The water never stops flowing here, from dusk to dawn. I hear it splashing against the bank. On the stone cut cap someone has written a small message in white paint: 'Don't Jump'.

I get to the main street. I pass the traffic lights, a post office, a supermarket, a clothes shop, a bank. I walk into the town square, cars parked around it.

I get to the statue in the centre. I stand by the square concrete base. There is a gold plate at the front inscribed with the words: 'J.M. Barrie 1757-1845 – "The Walker"'. I look up at the bronze sculpture. I can see the outline of the boots, the jacket, the big bag on the back, the hat on top. The arms are outstretched. The wall lights of the town hall behind shine against the statue and the head is a black shape as I look up. But I always imagine The Walker is smiling.

I pull my bag off my back. I sit on the concrete base. I look down the street. I have the freedom of the town. There's always sticky people around the city. But not out here at night.

I've walked ten miles on the dual carriageway. But I feel like I could walk forever. I stand. Better not to sit for too long. Hard to get going again. I bend each leg. I rub the backs of my thighs and calves. I'll have to get new boots for the winter.

I walk down the main street to the traffic lights. They change every thirty seconds, even though there's no drivers to come and go. Changing colours all night to an empty street. Awful waste of electricity really. I go up close to them. The lights are just circles of coloured full stops. I stare at the amber when it comes. It means prepare to stop. It reminds me of the torch beam yellow. I walk back up the street and sit under The Walker.

I pull off my shoes and socks. I wiggle my toes and stretch them out. I take off my high-viz jacket. The jumper with 'Champion' written across the front. The check shirt. The vest. I sit in my skin. It's good and cold. I look around. Not a sinner, not a sound. I scratch an armpit. I walk out to the middle of the main street. The road is wet on my feet. I stand on the white line in the centre. I flex my biceps. After a minute, I let off a roar. The silence falls again in the town. I let off another roar, louder. I'm coughing after this one. Heart thumps. A light comes on somewhere.

I go back to the statue. I put on the vest, the check shirt, the 'Champion' jumper, the high-viz jacket, the socks and the old leaking boots. I put my bag on my back.

I walk by the bank, the clothes shop, the supermarket, the post office. I stop at the traffic lights. I look to the town square. I can see The Walker, the arms outstretched. Smiling down at me. I smile back.

The walk is always easier on the way back to the city. A car whizzes by outside the suburbs. Boxy lads squeezed inside, music beating, a purple light shining from the underbelly. They circle the little roundabout a few times. Then they zoom back by me toward the town. They beep as they pass. Sticky people. I shouldn't be walking out here at night. But I live with risk.

As I walk across the motorway bridge, I see her leaning against the crash barrier. She is looking up at me. The only trouble with the motorway is there is no cover. But usually there is no need to hide.

There is nowhere to turn off on the slip road. I have to keep going toward her. I don't let on to see her at all. I keep my eyes down on the sparkling tarmac. But as soon as I set foot on the hard shoulder, I hear her say 'Excuse me?' I say nothing. I keep walking. She has the torch in her hand. It shines on the road. But she could flash it in my face, if she wanted.

'Excuse me?' she says again. I'm close by now. She says it so loud I couldn't miss it. Unless I was deaf. But that could be dodgy to pull off. I stop. 'Yes?'

'Did you pass by here a while ago?'

'Pass by? Where? Here?'

'Yes.'

'No. No, I wasn't this way before. Not for a long time.'

'I thought I saw you pass by earlier. From my camp.' She nods back to the bog, 'I thought it was you.'

'No. That wasn't me.'

'You don't normally pass this way?'

'No.' I look back toward the town. 'My car broke down. Back there. In the town. But there's no one about. I'm going to the city. To get help.'

'That's awful, can it be fixed?'

'What's that?'

'Your car, can it be fixed?'

'I don't know. I don't know much about cars.'

'Can you ring anyone?'

'I don't have a phone. I don't use them.'

'I'd give you mine, but the battery is flat.'

'That was it.'

'What?'

'The battery. In the car. It's flat.'

'You poor thing. There wasn't a phone box in the town?'

'Vandalised. I must be on my way.' But I've hardly gone two steps and she calls me again.

'Excuse me! Really sorry to bother you when you have enough trouble, but I'm very stuck, and I wonder, do you, by any chance, have such a thing as a tin-opener? Maybe in your bag there?'

'A tin-opener?'

'Yes.'

'You need to open a tin?'

'Yes, do you have one?'

'I do.'

'Great! Could I borrow it? Just for a couple of minutes?'

She has a funny accent. She's not local. Her voice is like the current under the bridge, where they tell you not to jump, she gets higher pitched, same as the water splashing against the sides of the bank, as she reaches the end of each sentence.

She must have grown up in a place hundreds of miles away from here. She picked up that twang in the schoolyard. Pushing, pulling, shouting, screaming. Bouncing balls, stones grazing your arms, a busted nose. I hated them places.

I pull off my bag from my back. Everything I need is within. Three pairs of trousers, three shirts, three changes of underwear, three pairs of socks, my wellingtons and a belt. Three cooking pots of different sizes, a frying pan, one knife, one fork and one spoon. A mug. A razor, a comb and a toothbrush. A shirt, tie, suit jacket and black shoes. A football jersey. My woolly hat. A bar of soap. A penknife with a tin-opener. Carrying all this around probably makes the walk harder. But I never leave anything in the hostel with the sticky people and their sticky fingers. 'You have a tin and no tin-opener?'

'Well, yes.' She could be smiling, but her face is a black shape in the streetlight.

'If you get the tin, I'll open it for you,' I say, taking out the penknife. 'There's a knack to this.' A penknife is a valuable item when you live in the bog. She might not want to give it back.

'Thank you so much!' She sounds young, but she could be old. She climbs over the crash barrier. I hear the boots squelching over the bog. I know they are boots by the stamp. I wonder where she bought them. I will ask her that before I go. The torch flashes out the opening, lighting up a part of the night. The tent looks to be of decent quality. I wonder where she bought it. But I'm not getting a tent.

When I move out of the hostel, I'll lie directly onto the bog. There'll be nothing separating me from the elements. It can get as cold as it wants. I hope it does. It's welcome to. It's surprising what the body can attune itself to. Strange machine really. If you ever built something as durable, you'd be minted.

But no one has yet. It's a long way off. I'll take full advantage of the skeletal and muscular structure I was born with in the meantime. Firm up the body. Away from all those racing sticky people. Nature is in no hurry. It's always on time.

If I fit with nature, I'll be alright. That's what they mean by staying fit. Fitting in with nature. Everything makes sense at night. You couldn't ever get your head straight during the noise of the day.

She's coming back now with a pile of tins in a plastic box. She must have strong arms. 'I may get a few opened while you're here. Do you mind?'

'No. I don't mind at all.' She takes out the tins and lines them up along the top of the crash barrier. I take the first one and clip the tin-opener onto the top. It bites into the rim. I wiggle the handle until it grips the little wheel. As I twist, it clicks around the circle.

'This is so great,' she says. An articulated lorry whizzes past. The gust lifts her hair high into the moonlight. There's a smell of oil and burning rubber.

The moon goes behind clouds. She shines the torch on the tin-opener. I look over to her. 'If you turn off your torch, I'll see better in the dark.'

'Really?'

'Once the eyes become accustomed.'

'Ah-hah.' She turns off the torch. I stop twisting the handle and the lid comes off. I can smell sweet fruit juice.

'Good man,' she says. She takes the opened tin from me and pours it into the plastic box. I start on the next one. 'Do you like peaches?'

'Peaches? Is that what these are?' I fiddle with the handle. The wheel catches and the teeth chew the rim. I guess she nods, her hair moves around her shape.

'They're not fresh fruit, but still they're good,' she says.

I get them all opened. I hand her the last one. She's happy. 'Thank you so much.'

'You're welcome.' I push the tin-opener back into the bottom of my bag.

'Would you like a bowl?'

'What?'

'Would you like a bowl of peaches?'

'No, thank you. I'd best be on my way. My car, you see.'

'Of course. Do you not like peaches?'

'What?'

'Do you not like peaches?'

'I do. I do like peaches.'

'Don't you want a bowl?'

'I'm not sure I'm that hungry.' I'm beginning to wonder if maybe she is a bit sticky after all. 'But where are the bowls?'

'Actually, I use mugs. They're back there. In my camp.' She points to the bog.

'I'd better not.'

'Come on! You're safe enough.' I guess she is smiling now by the rise of her voice. 'What's your name?'

'What?'

'Your name?'

'My name is Jeremiah.'

'Of course it is. Come, I'll get you a mug of peaches for all your hard work.' She climbs over the crash barrier. She carries the box of peaches to the tent. She is fit enough. You have to be to live in the bog. Her boots squelch. She stops at the tent and turns. 'Come.

I climb over the crash barrier. My old boots sink. The ground is soft. It wasn't the best spot to pitch up. With no tin-opener and no bowls. People get very confused. But that's because of the day.

She has gone inside the tent. I stop at the entrance. 'Welcome to my camp!' she says. Her voice sounds different in there. She's kneeling on a sleeping bag. There are lengths of beads hanging everywhere, all different colours. Some are wooden but most are plastic.

She has the torch set up in the corner. She has two mugs on a small wooden table. They are three-quarter full with peaches in fruit juice. The plastic box with the rest is now covered with a lid, beside a pile of folded clothes. 'Are you coming in, Jeremiah?'

'No. I'm fine here.' I kneel at the edge of the floor cover.

'Fair enough.' She hands me the mug. It's a fisherman's tin. They use them mainly for worms as far as I know. Good for little else. Burn the lips off you if it were hot. But it's not. It's ice cold. Pieces of peach float around in the juice. I sip it. It's sweet. I suck up one of the peach segments, making a slurping sound, breaking the silence of the night. 'Sweet, aren't they?'

'They're good. Not like fresh fruit. But not bad.'

'Not many peach trees around here, Jeremiah.'

'Not many.'

She sips the juice. 'I don't suppose you have anything to smoke?'

'No.'

'Pity.'

'Are you going to be here long?' I say. I'll have to change my route by the looks of this. Get new boots for the winter and get off the motorway. Take the old road.

'It depends. I don't make plans anymore.'

'That's about the best plan,' I say. She slugs the mug. I look around the tent. There's a pillow with blue strawberries on the case and a photo sellotaped to cardboard on top. There are two children in the photo. Beside the pillow, there's an alarm clock with two silver bells on the ears. The woman keeps track of time.

I finish the mug. 'Thanks.'

'Thank you so much for the use of your tin-opener.'

'You're welcome to it. I better be going. My car.'

'Of course.'

I hand her the empty mug. 'Hope to see you this way again, Jeremiah,' she says and shakes my hand. She doesn't let go. I don't know what to do. Her hand is warm. I couldn't say what age she is. She's not that young. She's not that old. Hard to say with women. They're not straightforward. Then she takes her hand away.

My old boots squelch on the bog as I walk back to the dual carriageway. The water seeps into my socks when I hit deep puddles.

I'll take the old road tomorrow night. The buck from down the country that says 'Kittle' told me it had been upgraded. New surface, yellow lines for the hard shoulder. Cat's eyes. Nearly as quick probably. There's no crash barrier on the old road. But I live with risk.

# SINGSONG

Christmas Eve. I stand on the hill by the Oscar Wilde on Friedrichstraße. Glasses clink as the last singsong dies. William streams into the snow. He stubs a cigarette as he zips up. See you later, he says. That'll do, I says. I never ask him where he goes. He'll be back, but when is hard to say. He went for a month once. I stayed at the Bahnhof. 24-hour security guards within 100 metres. Call the Schutzpolizei if there was trouble. Blast of the air con, a blessing in the November cold, a gift in the July heat. I played on the street on my own. One-man-band. Takings were well down. William kept the melody straight. But takings didn't rise when William came back. I watch him walk down to the Mehringplatz. If I followed, he'd get mad. He doesn't want me following him. Unless he calls me. I'm used to him going and coming now. He needs to go. He needs to be solo at times. Every man does. Snow all over the place, the roofs, the log cabins of the stalls, the tree branches along the streets weighed down with the ice. The sky blacker as I look up. Clouds blocking the star lights, the moon. The city bright makes it darker. Door whines in the Oscar. A lady laughs. We're all in there. A big spill tonight. It'll take the bottle boys hours to clear the place. The old country rules in the city of time. Here the bus comes five minutes early, even at this hour, the carriage full of emptiness. Buses are never late in Berlin. Early is easy. But me and William don't get on any buses. No timekeeping where we come from. We use a while, around and ago. Hours, minutes, seconds in this land. But we're not really from the old place no more. No time for waiting. I start to walk, boots crunch in the snow. I pull together my jacket. I find a bootlace in my pocket, the very thing. Tie up as best as I can. Air is cold. Golden heat from the streetlights. I hear other footsteps. I stop. Footsteps continue. Footsteps are real. I turn and see two men up the hill. Arms over shoulders. Wobbling. Relief flows like William's piss melting into the snow. The pair trip, their shapes shadowing ahead of them. They see me. They speak to each other at the same time, neither listening to the other. They walk and talk. They reach and pass by. They turn down Reinhardtstraße. Street is quiet again. Lights of the season flickers. Colours of the old country. Red and green. Haven't seen those green fields and red heather for decades. Never will again. I become sick one day in the closest city to home three decades later. Die after a few days lying on a trolley in a hospital corridor. But not now. The future in the present. Giant tree in the Mehringplatz. Draped in lights. Topped with a star and an angel. Neck stiffens as I look up. The Angels' eyes are blue. The glasses William gave me are catching snowflakes on the lens. I take them off. William found them on the seat at the bus stop. Good find they were. I can see with them. Einfach Klasse! Wipe them with my sleeve. I put them back on. Much worse now. Edges are softer. But I like the world in this vision. I leave them as they are and move on. Don't need to see all that well anyway. I've seen enough. I look back up Friedrichstraße. Lights flicker. I crunch on by the giant tree. Music jingles all the way. I pass the wooden huts of the Weihnachtsmarkt. At the centre of the Mehringplatz, there is a fountain. It spills water from the mouth of a stone carved angel with wings. It drips to a motte all around. Water pours all day and all night. The noise of dripping is soothing. I sit on the concrete surrounds. I pull up my sleeve and reach into the ice-cold water. The floor of the motte is carpeted with pfennigs. I take enough for a Laugenstangen and Schwarzkaffee from the Bahnhof Café in the morning. Somebody else's wishes come true. I only ever take a few coins. Too much and the Stadtrat will cover it with mesh, William keeps saying. You'll get the pfennigs in but not out. They did that to us in Munich. Leave something for the next man in boots and string anyway. At the top I'll see the whole city. I'll get to the Park Platz easy from

98

there. Think of William as I climb the hill. William never tells me where he goes. I never ask. Maybe some day I will ask him. And maybe he will tell me. But not now. I don't want to know tonight. Music jingles all the way. Louder by the wooden stalls. Special shops for the season. All shut for the holidays until the 26<sup>th</sup>. Start work again. Survival easier in our line of business when economy is open. Our business dead on Christmas Day. Clock chimes. Time is King in this country. Everything comes early. Early is easy. William and I were born late. Different in different lands. Time zones. Christmas Day in Kiritimati on Christmas Island doesn't come until 13 hours after Berlin. Christmas came 12 hours before Berlin in Baker Island. Berlin is even an hour ahead of our old land. William got me a book once in the Weihnachtsmarkt about it.

The Park Platz. That's where I need to be. The place I love to go. The last space. The Fiat. All the wheels long taken. Hubs rusted over. Just four circles of metal. You can't even see the original nut holes. But I'm the only one that looks. Back window long gone. You can see behind you more clearly. Fiat left here since 1988. Fahrzeugschein is the date stamp. The past in the present. It's a present for me. The Fiat. I climb in the back window. Wet and cold. But free and safe. Relatively. I pull out the folded newspaper from my jacket that I'd taken from the Bahnhof Café bin. The Fiat seats are red leather. Fluff busted through at the seams. I use the old words to dry the seat. Put the sheets under me. Breaking news now breaking cold. My nose is frozen. Red-nosed for the jolly season. I take out my steel flask. Twist off the lid. Take a bolt. Sweet sour sharp. Blood into cheeks. Warmth in heat. Waiting for it all day. A release. Comfort good enough to make being alive worth it. Almost. Then it's gone as quick. Put lid back. Put flask into jacket. I lie. Crinkle of news smashes silence. William trudges elsewhere. He doesn't like the Fiat. No room to stretch his longer legs. I am a foot shorter. A foot wider too.

You wouldn't ever think we came from the same stock. But I am less cramped in the Fiat. I still have my foot against the back side window. Toes cold. Springs pierce through the newspaper. Not much foam left. Like my jacket. Morning getting close. Eyes shut. Christmas presents. Under the lovely Christmas tree, with bells, and tinsel and an angel with blue eyes and a star at the very top, jostling to be the one we all looked up to. The angel won, for talk's sake, in case anyone came. The angel always wins. But the star was up there too. William and I run barefoot in pyjamas to the sitting room, to the tree. William finds a little snooker table. We'd begged for one after the black ball world final we'd watched on the black and white TV. When the legs broke we put it on the kitchen table. We lost some of the balls. The black and the blue. William blamed me. We started using marbles. We lost some of the marbles. The red mixed with white and the green mixed with orange. The cues got broken in a fight. I wanted to play swords. William started using the sweeping brush to pot the marbles. But it wasn't very accurate. Should never have used the cue as a sword. But I didn't like the game of snooker. It looked easy when we watched it on the TV. But it wasn't easy at all. The balls wouldn't go in. I started pushing them in with my hands, pretending I potted them, imagining I was making century breaks. It was the start of fantasy. I had to play on my own for this game. I didn't want to play with William anymore. I didn't want to tell William that. He would have been disappointed if I had told him. But I couldn't see any of the pockets when I was taking a shot. I had no glasses. Eyesight weakening even then. We lost the rest of the marbles and the balls. William was outraged. Speeding thoughts of William. Where is William now? Sleep not coming. Breathe. Air cold. Steam comes out my mouth. Chest is radiator of warm air. I adjust position. Not more comfortable. Even less so. Should have stayed still. But I can't find the place I was before. Face to Fiat front. Two seats. Headrests watch me.

Like the blacks of an eyeless skull. Ghosts beyond of many passengers. Years of conversations across the gear stick. Laughter. Cries. Shouts. Bad directions. Couples. Parents with a child on the back seat. Madmen with an empty car and a full trunk. The present in the past. Sleep closer. Sleep falls. Hardy bucks in this cold. Used to it. Sleep anywhere now. Mild satisfaction as I drift. Dreams of back and forth. Past, present, future. Tense. Histories and mysteries. The Park Platz by the Mehringplatz. Snow falling gently on the roof. I get to my old dream, same dream I have for years. Three figures from an ancient time, maybe thousands of years ago, before writing or reading was invented, maybe even before the wheel, before people thought. But these figures did think. They sit in a cave on a hill. They are trying to decide what to do with some very important thing. I can never figure out what the thing is. Everyone in the world wants it. I want it too. I badly want it. It kills me not knowing what the thing is. No one will take it if they are given it, one of the figures says. They will have to find it. But if they find it, another says, they will not want it. They will throw it away. The three figures think about this for a while. The best thing to do, the third one says, is to put it somewhere they will never find it. If we put it somewhere they will never find it, they will spend their whole time looking for it. Then they won't find it. But that's right, the first figure says, because if they find it, they won't want it and it will perish. Agreed, the second figure says. But where do we put it? The three figures think about this for a while. I have an idea, the second one says eventually. If we put it in the very bottom of the sea, beyond all the fish and shell-life and sea plants, underneath the seabed. There is no way any of them will ever find it there, the second figure says. They think about this for a while. I can't agree, the third says then. They are very clever. Someday, in a future we can only dream of now, here in our simple cave, believe it or not, they will have inventions that can go beyond all the fish and shell-life and sea plants, down to the depths of the sea. Contraptions with navigational systems and special tools for digging up even the seabed. It will take a long time, but they will eventually find it and we will be lost. You are right the first one says. We cannot put it there. They think again for a while. I have an idea, the third one says. I think we should shoot it out into space. There is no way they will ever get into the deepest, darkest reaches of space, beyond all of the moons and the planets and all of the stars and suns, to the furthest reaches of the universe. We should put it there. That is what we must do. They think about this for a while. I can't agree, the second one says. As my friend said before, they are ingenious. And if you are right that they will eventually concoct a way to get down to the deepest parts of the ocean, beyond all the fish and shell-life and sea plants, travel the seabed and dig it up and find it there, well, there is no reason to think that, believe it or not, the finest minds will not  be clever enough, in many centuries in the future,  to concoct a way to rise like a majestic bird to the skies and beyond to the great blackness of the infinite night, to all of the moons and the planets and all of the stars and suns, to the deepest, darkest reaches of outer space, the furthest linings of the universe, and find it there, with some incredible technology we can only ever dream of in our lifetime.  They think about this for a while. You are right, the first one says. But where do we put it? Is there nothing we can do, nowhere we can put it that they won't find it?  The second figure did not know. The third figure did not know. The three figures became disconsolate. They sat in silence, meditating for a long time. In the end, the first figure said, I have an idea. I know somewhere we can put it that they will never, ever find it in a million years, not before the end of time itself. And where is that? the second one said. Yes, that would be interesting to know your solution, my friend, the third one said. What we can do, the first one said, is put it inside them. They will never find it there. The three figures all agreed. I could never figure out what the thing was they were trying to hide.

Snow falls gently on the roof of the Fiat. Soft on the tin. Door hinges somewhere. Oscar Wilde far down the street. Dog barks. Step of foot. Nearby. Eyes open. Sleep broken again. New threat. Newspaper crinkles. Look out glassless back window. Cold night against cheeks. Three drunks on a bench in the Park Platz. Drunk and happy. Not dangerous. But they don't see me. I pull out flask. Take a slug. Blast of heat. Red cheeks. Heat dies. Put away flask. Night of Oscar Wilde in head. Singsong. William with guitar. Too packed for security to usher us away. Accordion on my lap. Claps of the local trade. The accordion and the guitar like bread and butter. Tea and milk. But they don't drink milk in the tea in this country. Or spread butter on bread. They take hot drinks black and pour oil on the crusts. We are outsiders.

Oscar Wilde better trade than the Bahnhof. Wet blow in from air con in winter. Dust in lungs in summer. Threat of theft. Turf wars with other practitioners. Awkward questions from the Schutzpolizei. Security Personnel eventually usher us away.  Small returns. Oscar Wilde pays us better. Security ignore us mostly. Except when owner is on premises. But usually pub is too packed then.

Only danger addicts know we collect. Made aggressive attempted withdrawal on occasion. But Oscar Wilde safer overall. Turn and turn about. No sleep. No wake. Cause by flask. Short heat at a price. Dawn soon. Night will be gone. The past sleeps by. The future will be present. Mixed-up. Eyes shut. Dreams dawn again. Now the future. Now the past. Now the present. Snow gentle on the roof.

Back in home town. Augustine Street. Cold weather. Damp. William sits across the table in our coffee shop. Not our coffee shop. We don't own the shop. We only own our instruments.

Drink coffee and scones here in good times. I tell William the coffee is good. William agrees. William examines guitar. Large hole in body. Stubs of lost strings hang on the pegs. My accordion is torn. Unplayed music escapes. Accordion fills with water on wet days. Tuning forks required in all departments. We sit at table. Keeping watch on the day. William looks at black coffee. Silent noise at table. Coffee girl brings William soya milk. Normal Tuesday at 4pm. I drink cow's milk in the coffee. Missed out on William's cosmopolitanism. William looks closely at neck of guitar. We are non-musical musicians. There are many such practitioners. Earning a living nonetheless. Or a dying. As the case may be. All earning out there this big day. The whole street. Adjust my chair. This is my regular chair at my regular table. In my regular coffee shop in my regular street. Augustine The Saint.

Same street. Same chair. Same table. Same coffee. Same accordion. Same time. Same day. Waitress changes. William has taken a single string from his pocket. He clips it to the peg on the saddle and draws it up the neck to the tuning keys. I tell him he needs to get a new set of strings. William does not like this advice. He smiles. We drink coffee. I tell William our sister has died. He nods. The funeral will be next Tuesday. I got word at the Post Office last Tuesday. Our addresses are fluid. Difficult for brother-in-law. William tightens the string, turning the tuning key. The sister's funeral will be in England. Her husband is English. The family is English. The husband is famous. Political politician. The husband could buy a million sets of new guitar strings. A million new accordions. If he wanted. But he doesn't want to. He is not a musician. Nether are we. But we continue to play nonetheless. We are non-musical musicians. We have this in common with brother-in-law. Sister went to London university. We abandoned school and joined musical tour. Tour's filtering threshold was low. Accordion and guitar practitioners. Not good idea. Failed and failing. Onward and downward. Sister has maids and butlers. Chandeliers. A golden turfbox. No newspaper blankets. No Fiat feet in the Park Platz. Simple things. The funeral. We are not going to the funeral in England. Surely not. Complicated business. Expense. William wants to go to the funeral. William tightens string around tuning key. Sound is odd. Our duty, William says. Coffee is cold. We take train and boat. Plane is cheaper nowadays. But we never flew. Not birds. Security hassles. Simple train. Simple boat. Simple things. We agree.

Non-musical musicians. Standing on the street. The present in the past. On Augustine Street. Shoppers pass by. Christmas. Just home from the Deutschland. Good calendar. Got us right. Raindrops glide down the decorated seasonal windows. Rolling on the smooth glass. Makes up shapes of things if you look long enough. Jaws. Noses. Eyes. The side of William's face and mine. Countries. England. Germany. Home country. Drawing the past, present and future within the frosted frames. Painting lives. Clear and coloured. And then fades toward the sill. To a line. Then to nothing. If you stare. Which I do.

      Loving couples pass by in warm soft boots with gloved hands together or naked fingers in each other's rear jean pockets. Sweet romance. Many other buskers at Christmas jolly. Amateur part-timers. Big time of the year. Tis the season to collect the lolly and the holly. Turf wars. But we get there early. Early watch on footpath avenue. 5am start. Early is easy. Good training in the Deutschland. No hassle. Simple rules. First there, first served. Set up on the cobbles. Three-hundred-year track. Worn to glass smooth. Ghost footsteps stare back at us. The past in the present. Buggies rattle by with newborns. Fruit of the loins in the rain dripping street. The future looks out over a milk bottle. Missed that bus. Fleshy pleasures off the menu after the music tour. We are side-by-side. Accordion cold in the grip. I press buttons, push and pull. Sounds come out. All together now.

Williams strums the guitar. Some strings attached. I press the keys of my accordion, squeeze the sides in and out. Harmony is quite off. Passers-by don't care. Not listening. Street is loud. See us and instruments and coffee cup. Sufficient for potential contribution. Play the old favorites. Come-all-ye. Not our favorites. Street's favourites. We don't have any favourites. Play another. Stand for our anthem. Stand for the music. We must like music after all these decades. Bubbles of rain on my glasses. Lens glisten. Marbling my vision to blurry blobs. William's sunglasses the same. William doesn't clean his. William does not wear sunglasses because of the sun. There is never any sun on Augustine Street. William has other reasons to wear sunglasses. Protective strategy. Avoid unnecessary recognition. We had to get out of town fast after music tour. A woman and guitar involved. We try a few anthems. Cup is empty. We don't have starter coins today. Or most days. An empty cup for our efforts. New threat. Youths running through street. One grabs the accordion. He breaks the strap across my shoulder. Other pulls the guitar off William. Slaps given to head. Kicks given to groin. Hole smashed in William's guitar. I freeze in the scrum, looking to the fresh torn chipboard edges. The gloss wood finish exposed as mulched-up glued chips. A large guitar, full of nothingness. The bundles of unplayed music spill out silently onto the street, escaping as William wrestles. Other youth plays tug-of-war with me and accordion. Rips hole in the top. Untapped tunes fly away. Youth laughs on street. I take him in headlock. I punch him in neck. Little effect. I am poor boxer. William gets the other on the nose. Face bloody. We are muscular non-musical musicians that day. Youths scoot away. Hole in guitar. Hole in accordion. Muscular non-musical musicians with non-musical musical instruments. We leave the city centre in disgust and walk along the salty promenade in the rain. Boots

106

leak. Wet sock on right foot. William not speak since youths came and went. William ten steps ahead. Rain gets heavier. William hurries further away. William becomes a blob in the distance. I try to keep up. Keep William in my sight. We keep walking. We leave the city far behind. We walk for days and nights. Rain comes for weeks. We pass through many towns. We pick up sustenance on the way. Few hours wash-up at restaurants. Free meal and cash. Short term. Wash-up liquid bad for William's guitar fingers. Staff complain of smell.

Learn to harvest scrap bins in restaurant backyards. Plenty of cold meat and vegetables. Cream and pie alright if separated from rice and pasta in congealed sauce. Sleep under bridges and in fields. Year becomes summer. Rain stops. Year becomes autumn. Rain starts. Winter. Christmas. Spring. Summer. Back in the city. We find charity shop. William finds new shoes for us. Not new. Dead men's shoes. Dead men's jackets, shirts, jumpers, trousers. Shopkeeper talks to William for a while. Shopkeeper gives William idea. William claps hands. Tells me idea, but it sounds complicated. William goes to another shop. William talks to shopkeeper at counter. William given boards. Two for me. Two for him. Ropes at tops of boards. Worn like a bib. Back and front covered. We wear on Augustine Street. Four hours contract daily. We stand where we played. Retired non-musical musical instruments in our bag nearby. Persons stop. Talk to each other. Read boards. Ignore us. We don't know if they go to shop afterwards. Or any other day. No job satisfaction. With music, audience nod head. Or tap feet. Or spit. Or curse. We return boards after four hours. Shopkeeper pays William. We eat at hostel. Boards good idea. But next day controversial. Youths try to steal boards. We fight, but we are weaker, worn from year of walking. Youths get away with boards. Police catch youths. Shopkeeper has no licence for boards on street. Policeman takes boards away from shop. Policeman asks William's name. Asks how to spell William. Policeman tells William name not on system. We are from country of red and green. We are ghosts. We were away for years. Policeman gives up and leaves. William goes to another shop. Easily gets more boards. We are experienced board-minders now. Other board-minders on street. But no turf wars. Payment guaranteed. Nights in hostel. Days on Augustine Street with boards. Simple things. Years pass by. A beautiful woman comes to Augustine Street. Hair waist length, straight and black. Eyes oval and large. I am in love. She has a board. But the board is not for advertising. She attaches white sheet to the board. Board is easel, we soon learn. Woman has a bag. She takes out pencil. She looks across at us on street with boards. But we are not beautiful. We do not look back. Woman places cap on cobbles. It fills faster than our cups. We should have a cap instead of a cup. We lost our caps a long time ago. Woman sketches on the sheet. We soon see the sketch is of two board-minders on Augustine Street. She completes the sketch. Now she takes out a palette. She squirts blobs of paint from tubes on the palette. She looks at us. Crowds of people stop and look at easel. Look at us. Shopkeeper will be pleased with the attention. She takes a brush. She looks at us. She dips the brush and fills in the sketch, colouring in the white spaces between lines. Green above the red. Old country colours. Good guess by the woman. Board-minders on sheet do not wear glasses. We can see their eyes. The eyes look at us. We look at them. William elbows me. He wants me to raise an exchange with the woman. An exchange of words.

Crowd stop and look at painting. The woman's cap fills with coins and notes. We might negotiate a fee for being the subjects. But I do not talk to artists. Artists are tricky. They do not always tell the truth. Or they tell it in the wrong order. We are artists. Of a sort. William elbows me again. The woman fills the bodies of the board-minders on her canvas. William kicks my knee. I say my prayers. William dances. William goes across the street to her. William circles her. She paints. William smiles at the cobblestones. No exchange takes place. Painful view. Some stop and read my boards. I call William back. We have work to do. William crosses over. Adjusts his boards. William elbows me. I say my prayers. I go across to her. The woman does not look at me. She is more beautiful at short distance. Painting is pretty in closer view. Two half-painted board-minders on a sketch of Augustine Street. They wear advertising boards and stand on smooth cobblestones. There is a bag of non-musical musical instruments on one side. I can see the broken pencil lines of the top of the stringless guitar. The gaping hole in the accordion. The woman knows detail. I weep by the cobblestones. I walk around the easel. William dances. I lie under the easel on the cobblestones. William laughs. Passers-by slow, look at me, point, laugh, then move on, not looking at the painting. Looking at me only. The woman continues to paint. She turns to William. She speaks to William. She walks across the street to William. She still holds her paintbrush and her palette. She takes off William's glasses. She smiles. William smiles, his eyes naked to the air. She dips the paintbrush in her palette, in the red blob of thick paint and she runs the paintbrush across William's face, a thick red streak. Rain falls. The rain runs onto William's red streaked face. Red drips off his jaw. I take off my glasses and look up at the sheet drawn on the easel. Raindrops hit my face, roll into my eyes. I blink, the world is glassy. The woman and William link arms. They dance, legs rising high in the air. Rain hits the woman's painting. The two board-minders on the canvas become smudges. Cloudy colours drip off the end of the canvas. Bubbles drop onto my face. Sour on my lips. I lie on the ground and salute.

Back on the road again. Just like the old times. Time still old. Along with us. William leads the way. Train journey over fields and flowing rivers. Silence in the music. Noise outside. We start to play a tune on the aisles for a sandwich. Scuttle for toilets when Ticketmaster appears. Oh what fun, dashing by the loo, in a one-legged open play, jingling all the way! But we weren't jingling any coins. Good old plan. The Big Smoke. William in a hurry. Slow down. I call him. Slow. Sister finished with the rush. Not going anywhere. Lies flat, mortally rigored. Hands in beads. Unless the other lost have converted her. Big wide streets in the capital. Higher buildings. An extra floor or two into the sky. Land cheaper in the air. Better markets here for buskers. Turf wars raise higher stakes though. We don't involve our tunes. Accents higher and lower pitch. Singy-song. Bus to the ferry port. Some controversy at terminal. Heckled about our patched-up non-musical musical instruments. William's sunglasses stare through the rain. Foot passengers on the ferry. William holds ferry tickets, talking to green-jacketed official. William gestures back to me. I scratch my withered head. Companions on a journey. William and me with wrong tickets. Confusion in the travel booking system. We missed out on real world modernization arrangements a long time ago. We were dreaming. Still dreaming, William and green-jacketed officials talk for a while. William weeps. Sister Act. Green-jacketed official starts shouting. William grips green-jacketed official. Wails. Green-jacketed official gets distracted. Appears to become interested in a distant corner of ferry. Green-jacketed official walks off. William nods sadly to me. We get on the ferry. Night hours of choppy water. Vast sea of the Irish. Stand on deck. Salty and biting. Look over the cross bar. A point for the old red and green. Wind in the thick darkness. Wary of the water. Lose something for ever down there in the sea. Never find it again. Me and William hoarders. Luckily we accumulated few goods to hoard. Veiled blessings. But could lose the glasses. No blind man will be King in the land of the two-eyed. I always wanted to be King. Stand back from the cross bar. Check glasses. They are still there. I can see the sea. We ply the lounge for the passing trade. Cup by feet. Serious need for caps. Non-musical musicians. Families pass by. A baby cries. I was a baby once. William too. Babies no more. Shapes of the past in the present. Times of youth and hunger. No more youth. But hunger still. Always hunger. At dawn William leads the way to the food area. No staff visible. Half past seven. Staff fill the bain-maries and take break before the breakfast rush. Old reliable stroke. Climb over barrier. Food smells good. Grab sausages. rashers, black and white pudding, stuff into jacket. Pastries off the sweet trolley. Opportunities may come only once today. Squash sweet sugary doughnut into mouth, yellow custard and whipped cream oozes. Sweetness injected into body. All together now. Hurray. Now hurry away. Comfort of filling up stomach. Warmth lifts. Accents of the singy-song behind. We get back on the deck. Salty freedom.

At the other side, we await to see same green-jacketed official. Sympathetic shaved-jaw side of beurocracy. But different green-jacketed team on appointment for disembarking foot passengers. Second chance Sunday for ferry company. On a Monday. Passenger tickets checked as they walk gangplank. About-turn to the toilets. Military style civilians. Wait until ferry empties. Boat gets quiet. Silent noises. Hoovers. Fans. Voices of the singy-song. Footsteps. Soon toilets will also be cleaned. We make our move. Race to the gangplanks. Dashing all the way, ho-ho-ho! Energizing exit. Free. Lift bottle of water in the Port Shop. Springy-song accents, taxi-ranks, yellow number plates. Hot fuel smell. William peels off notes for taxi-driver. No stroke pulled here. Unusual status, having notes. Coins the staple we deal in for decades. Never notes. Unless in Rome. When in Rome do as the Romans do. We were eternal millionaires in that city. Driver looks at the notes. Looks at us. Looks at the address. Grunts. He opens all the windows in the taxi. We get in. Feel like royalty. Leather seats. Sign says no feet on seats. We take our feet down. Driver glides out road through neat square fields. Thatched roofs with white houses behind black lines. Drive for hours. We get to granite pillars and electronic gates. Silver post box. William does not know key code. Driver wants to press intercom. We do not allow this. We get out. William tells driver to return in three hours. Driver nods and leaves. We climb the wall by the gates. Walk through many tall trees. We get near mansion. Long drive up. I count 24 windows. Chimneys with cowls. Stables to rear. Many large cars. Autumn leaves. At back of stables, large tent. Marquee. TV cameras. BBC. SKY. Bowler-hatted persons on horseback. Suited mourners. White tablecloths in marquee. Glasses clink. We stand watching from distant trees. Soft music. Violin and flute players on a stage inside. We watch them play through clear plastic windows. William smiles. Politicians get out of smooth limousines. Noise in sky. Helicopter. We hide under bushes. Helicopter lands on grass. Royalty get out of helicopter. From the cover of *Hello!* magazine in the bin in the café on Augustine Street. Royalty shake hands with brother-in-law. Brother-in-law wears black tie. Niece and nephew nearby. Babies last time we met. Only time we met. William brought them German chocolate. January of Christmas. Lost good calendar that year. Christmas all year round in the Oscar Wilde. Left Berlin in a hurry. Controversy on Friedrichstraße. We should have brought a metal lorry toy to them. Last longer than chocolate. Country estate crowded. Not our scene. William weeps. We walk back to gates. Wait for taxi.

Christmas Day. Sunlight shines on the soft snow. White season to be jolly. Awakening. First failure of the day. I stand stiff. I have cold Fiat feet. I am against the grain in the past, present and future. I look out at the entrance to the Park Platz. Green and red lights of the old country flicker everywhere. Cold rises. Church doors bolted shut. Midnight mass hours ago. Times ahead of carols and rhymes. Mistletoe and wine. Time difference still niggling, a discomfort. Christmas Day at a different time in one place to the next. Which is the right time to be in? Forthcoming glory of the Bratwurst with mustard. Bird-like voices of the worshippers from the church will fill the straßen. Services. Genuflect. Stand. Kneel. Sit. Kneel. Stand. Genuflect. Then leave. Nourished. But not us. No church tile darkened with our shadow for decades. Pray in the mind. I will bless the food later. In the Berlin Korps. William will come back. He always has. He always will. He is my brother-in-arms. Sister will marry in the New Year. William will leave me alone in Berlin. He goes to Finland. A job from the beery bird-slinger operatives in the Oscar Wilde on Friedrichstraße. With the Finns in the High North. Picking berries off the winter trees. Promise of markkaa, short hours, steak teas, topless bronzed blondes in steam pine saunas every evening. But hours long, markkaa minimal, evenings of cat food and wet leaves in rotting cabin near a blocked sewer. Today Bratwurst Christmas lunch in the Berlin Korps warehouse in Kuglerstraße. Bier in wrinkled tankard. Sharpens the World View. Dry snow on glasses as I walk. Settling.

Lying on the corner of Augustine Street. Face of William streaked in red from the woman's brush flick. William beats his advertising board unmelodically. He misses the strings on his guitar. I miss the keys of my accordion. I lie still under the painting. Glasses in my hand. I watch William and the woman link arms and join in song and dance. They salute the street. I salute. Raindrops roll down the painting, making a crooked rainbow on the sheet, over the smudged non-musical musicians and their non-musical musical instruments. All the green and red of our old country dripping off the edge of the canvas. Green rolls onto my face. Into my naked eyes. Vision blurs. I try to sing.

# THE OLD MAN ON THE HILL

The old man waited on the hill. The grass had now grown up to the knees of his trousers. He adjusted himself on the flat stone. The dandelions danced in the breeze. The sun was low in the western horizon, a pale semi-circle. Swallows lifted *en masse* from the leaves of the giant beech tree by the cow house. The old man looked to his right, to Malachy's house at the end of the road. There was a Volkswagen Golf parked at the front of the bungalow. A mountain bike was resting by the back door. There were patches of moss in the hollows of the orange-brown clay roof tiles. The curtains were still pulled behind the teak windows. Within the house, Malachy and his wife slept together on a double bed. They snored. In another room, Malachy's son dreamt of girls as he lay underneath posters of football teams. Across the road, Paddy Reilly's shop was boarded up. There were lines of rusting gas cylinders along the border wall, two fuel pumps at the centre of the elevated forecourt. The shop inside had lines of empty shelves, boxes on the counter, the cash register drawer was open, the plastic tray empty. The old man's eyes moved right again, tracing the twisting networks of roads and boreens he could see from his position. He could see the humps and hollows that flooded in the winter, the clay tiles which marked out each house in the village. The old man knew most everyone living within his sight, he knew most of their parents, most of their grandparents, a whole history unfolded across the shapes and colours of the landscape before him, faces, voices, memories, christenings, communions, confirmations, weddings, stations, funerals. Many of the houses had haysheds, some rising sharp to an apex, others curved and soft in a half-moon, all painted in the cheapest colour, red. Some of the haysheds had built on lean-tos for hay turners, others extensions with more modern, galvanised roofs, tractors and jeeps parked nearby. To his far left, the old man could see the stone facade of The Laughing Horse Inn, the red door shut, the antique lamps hanging extinguished within. Behind, a grassy mound that was once known as Yates' Well.

The village was perfectly still, like a painting. But the old man did not paint. To the left of the beech tree, in the foreground of the cow house, was Malachy's hayshed, where he always parked his tractor, a Massey Ferguson 35. At the foot of the hill, there was a cubicle house. It had been built over the course of one day in May, in a steel frame, the girders and sheets tacked together by a team of men from down the country, the old man's wife bringing a teapot of strong tea and a plate of her famous apple and rhubarb pie, decorated with a flowery tea towel, in the middle of the afternoon. The old man and Malachy had concreted the floors of the cubicle house, built up the walls and fitted steel cubicles in their time over the following summer. The walls had stopped two foot short of the roof eaves. At one side of the yard, to the right of the cubicle house, three half-moon feeders were positioned. The remainder of the winter silage was in a small pile in the corner of the pit afore the cubicle house. To the left of the cubicle house, after the dungstead, where the muck was pushed each week by Malachy's son in the tractor, idly rocking his head to an invisible beat, there was a large quarry, a crater covered in weeds and small stones. There was a small pile of chippings by the gate to the road. It was the last limestone that could be got out of the site. Further down the road, at the head of a boreen, was the old man's house. It was a little larger than Malachy's. Malachy had built his house during a severe recession, when houses were restricted in size by state-sponsored mortgages. But the old man's house had been built by his father-in-law, Donald, with notes stuffed in a mattress from fields sold to Mike Feerick and the house had not been subject to any regulations. Pink paint peeled off some of the old man's house now, moss grew on the slated roof. There was a small extension by the asbestos-roofed turf shed, which had a toilet, a scullery, a back kitchen and a bathroom. Within the house, the old man's wife sat in the big kitchen, by the range, at the steaming kettle. She had her legs crossed, scratched her jaw and counted '18,19,20'. Her mixing bowl, spoon and measuring jug lay on a shelf in the scullery in the extension. The old man's wife did not make soda bread, or rhubarb and apple pie, not now, not anymore. But one day the old man's wife had done this and for many other days. Every morning, she had taken out the enamel bowl and the flour and the butter she had churned from the milk from the cow in the cow house, she had taken the free range eggs she had gathered in the straw at the henhouse beyond the water tank, behind the turf shed, where the hens did not pick and squawk, not now, not anymore. One day and many other days, the old man's wife had used her cold hands to gently break up the butter into two cups of flour in the bowl, until it was all like a fine breadcrumb mix, keeping working her hands high over the bowl, aerating the mix, as she had been taught to in Donald's little cottage at the corner of the boreen, before her mother died in the stone cottage now used as a sheep pen by Malachy. When the old man's wife had shook the mixture into fine breadcrumbs, she would break three eggs into half a cup of sugar, then she would stir the mixture and add it to the centre of the breadcrumb mix. She would then gently, very, very gently, mix the pastry together in her special way, feeding the breadcrumbs with a fork into the eggs and sugar and then stirring with her wooden spoon, and then kneading with her hands. She would then tip the pastry out onto her floured table, dusting it with more flour, and she would roll the pastry with her rolling pin. She would flatten it into a smooth circle, she would leave it in a bowl in the scullery, covered with a damp cloth overnight and she would take another pastry she had made the day before. She would roll this pastry out. She would

116

butter a plate with a small brush. Then she would slice the pastry in half with her breadknife and drape one half over the plate. She would trim the pastry around the edges of the plate with a toothless dinner knife and fork the base. She would have apples from the orchard down the boreen and rhubarb from the garden and she would peel the apples and chop off the flesh into the pie and then clean the rhubarb and chop into the apples and then sprinkle it all with sugar. She would wet the edges of the pastry base with cold water, sprinkled off the tips of her fingers. She would then cover the fruit with the rest of the pastry. She would trim the edges with the toothless knife. She would fork the edge of the pie and decorate the top with apple and rhubarb shapes of pastry. She would pierce holes in the pastry crust to let steam escape during baking. She would brush the pie with a beaten egg. She would bake it in a hot oven as she washed her bowl and cups and forks and spoons and knives and jugs. The pie would be cooked in less than an hour if the range was hot.

The old man's wife would give the old man a slice of pie in the evening after his boiled egg. If Mike Feerick passed by and stopped, he would also be given a slice of the pie. When Malachy visited the house with his son, while they were herding or doing some other job on the farm and they were taking a short break, they too would be given a slice of the pie. The pies made by the old man's wife were known to be particularly well-made. As a younger woman, she had made many pies for many people in the village, they would bring her whiskey and sweets in return at Christmas and Easter. She had been taught to bake by her mother. But the old man's wife did not bake now, not anymore. And the old man did not get a slice of apple pie after his boiled egg in the evening, not anymore. Further down the boreen, at the corner was Donald's old house. It was now a stone barn with no roof, wild weeds grew through the window shapes. Further on, the old man could see Mike's house. Mike's tractor was parked at the front, several black cats prowled the garden. Mike sat inside, eating an egg. Music blared over a mirror with a photo of Elvis Presley on the wall. The hill where the old man sat was at the corner of a large square of lime and yellow fields bordered with stone walls and hawthorn bushes, streams and clumps of various trees. He could tell where North, South, East and West were from his position. The sun rose in the morning in the west. It rose high into the sky and went around toward the south. Then it set in the East. It never went to the North. But the old man was not so simple in his thinking to believe that it was the sun that moved, even though that was how it seemed to the simple-minded. The old man was aware that it was the earth that moved and not the sun. But he also knew that as the earth circled the sun, the moon circled the earth. They all moved together, circling each other simultaneously in their various precise ways. Sun, moon and Earth were all sphere-like, as far as the old man could tell. It was strange then, the old man thought, that there were only a few other spheres that existed in the world in such a perfect way that had not been created by man. The sun and the earth worked together to determine the length of the days, the seasons and the years. Even though the old man's first day was the same length as the one he now lived in, they did not seem to be the same to him. The days all seemed to move very fast now. The old man moved very slowly in these fast days. He tried to look up at the sun, but it was too bright to stare. For a second, he could see the outline, a golden disc. Around the sun, the sky was blue. There were some clouds at the edge. Everything was still. It seemed that the old man was at the centre of everything. But the old man knew he was not at the centre of anything. He had not been at the centre on his first day, even though it had seemed he was, and he would not be at the centre of anything on his last. He had not always known this. He had moved away from thinking he was at the centre of the world as he had grown.

The grass in the fields around him were tinted white with morning frost. But the spring sun was melting the white without movement. The old man could not see the heat of the sun, but he could feel it. The collie by the old man's boots twitched its tail. It lay its black and white head on white paws, the jaws were slightly drooped, eyes half-open. Across from the old man's position, he could see onto the roof of the cubicle house. At the apex, a grey starling had begun the construction of a nest.

The old man watched the starling push a twig with its tiny beak against a piece of muck on the galvanized sheet. The twig fell to the ground. The starling flew over to the tree and pulled at the leaves. It returned with another twig some moments later, a twig with two tiny green leaves sprouting at the side. But the green buds would grow no more now they had been separated from the tree. This twig stuck to the muck. The starling fluttered its wings, rising over the shed, twittering and flying back to the beech tree, where it tore against the branches. This time it took a leaf and carried it across to the nest-under-construction. The old man reached for his pipe. He pulled it out and inspected the pot. He tapped it on the flat stone and inspected it again. The collie was looking up, its eyes were open, its jaw low, its tongue hanging out.

'Will we have a smoke?' the old man said to the dog. The collie whined. The old man took out a plastic pouch which contained an ounce of *Old Holborn*. He fingered the tobacco and pushed it into the pot, pressing it down with his thumbs, before adding more. When the pot was full, he put the plastic pouch into his jacket pocket. He took out a box of matches. He put the stem of the pipe into his mouth. He caught the matchbox in the palm of his left hand and held a match in the thumb and finger of his right, cupping both with the rest of his fingers against the gentle morning breeze. He struck the match, just then moving his pipe pot to the centre and touched the tobacco with the flickering flame. The pot glowed red. The old man drew smoke and air through the stem into his lungs, where it circulated and then drifted back out between his lips. Thick grey clouds rose. The starling pushed more tiny twigs in between the leaves and muck in the apex of the cubicle house roof, using its beak and claws.

The old man rested the smouldering pipe against his knee as he watched the starling work. The old man knew years of smoking had weakened his heart. They had told them smoking was good for a man once. Now it was said to shorten a life. Over-exertion at the old man's age could be fatal, the doctor had said one day, as he ran his fingers down his silken tie in an office with a potted plastic plant and a humming computer. One day, the old man might lose the walk. One day, he might not be able to breathe. But that day was not today. The old man looked at his watch. It was a quarter to nine.

The day was drifting by. The foundations for a concrete trough at the side of the cubicle house had been dug weeks earlier. The old man looked at the stripped trench. Malachy had been told by an agricultural inspector that calves thrived better eating from a concrete trough and there was a grant to build one. It was also easier with a concrete trough to ensure all of the calves got the same amount of nuts. The last winter, they had scrambled each evening to the steel troughs in the centre of the yard, as Malachy's son poured out the bag. The stronger always got the most of the meal. The old man looked at the three half-moon feeders. The calves also thrived better being forked barrows of silage. The two-year-old bullocks on the other side chewed their way through the pit, their progress moderated by an electrified wire across it, which Malachy adjusted weekly. The muck was scraped away into a dungstead every Saturday. Malachy would transport box the muck into the fields around the cubicle house each summer. Chemicals would flow into the adjoining effluent tank.

A tractor started. The old man looked left, to the boreen, to Mike's house. Mike was in his tractor. Smoke billowed from the tall grey exhaust pipe over the engine of the Massey Ferguson 135. The old man watched the red tractor travel out onto the boreen. Black cats ran in all directions. He could hear Mike rev the engine gently as the large black wheels turned, the grey discs came into view, they had little black slots on the rim, which gave the big back wheel a sly smiling expression as it turned. Mike drove past Donald's old house and stopped at the end of the boreen, by the old man's house. Then Mike turned right. He drove past the quarry, looking into it, at the weeds, as he passed, then he looked left to the boarded-up windows of Paddy Reilly's shop. As Mike reached the beech tree, he looked to the cow house, the hay shed, the cubicle house and up the hill to the old man. Mike saluted. But the old man did not respond. The collie had sat up, his tail twitching. He growled, tongue hanging out, black eyes wide. 'Easy,' the old man said. Mike stopped at the junction by Malachy's house. He turned right and drove the tractor down the road, revving the engine more now, then turning the corner and passing The Laughing Horse and Yates' Well. It was said that when The Laughing Horse was built in the 1600s, the water from the well was used to make the beer sold at the Inn. But no pub made its beer anymore. The old man looked to the blue sky. A white dot traveled across. The old man watched it. The collie lifted its head and twitched its tail, its mouth open. The old man knew the white dot he watched carried hundreds of people within it, some watching a television-like device, some eating chocolate, some drinking beer. The old man had been on an aeroplane once. A trip to England to attend Brendan's funeral, the husband of his wife's sister, Philomena. The journey was far smoother than on any train or ferry. The supreme power of the engine as it accelerated on the massive wide runway lifted them high into the sky. The old man had enjoyed it. The clouds were white and fluffy underneath as they floated across to England at a thousand miles an hour. The old man had been to England many times, but only once by aeroplane.

The old man's father had no land and worked as a carpenter. When the old man's father was in his late thirties, he had secured a contract to build state houses for rural people. The old man had gone to work for his father from the age of ten. The year the old man flew to England, Brendan's son, Stephen, had collected him from the airport. Stephen was tall and spoke with a smooth accent. They travelled through the city in a new Mercedes. Stephen spoke on a mobile telephone. Stephen pointed out blocks of flats that he owned. They had a family dinner in Stephen's house, a mansion with electric showers, *en suites*, a snooker room with a bar, a large garden, automatic gates, a long leafy avenue. The old man had drank pints of stout that night in a pub called The Butcher and Boy. There were not many mourners at Brendan's funeral. But that was normal in England. Brendan lay flat and grey in the coffin, eyes shut tight, hard cold hands entwined. There was no priest for any blessing. Philomena said some words without tears. Then the remains were moved on a conveyor belt through a curtain of rubber strips to the ferocious heat beyond. There the coffin was incinerated. The ashes were handed to Philomena in a little black pot as they left, the smell of burnt bones in the air outside. The old man knew he would not see England again. He was too old to travel anywhere now, anymore. He did not know when he had become too old. One day he could travel. The next he could not. He grew tired of sitting on the stone. He pulled out the stem of his pipe once more and he dragged on it, billows of smoke soon lifted into the morning. He put the smouldering pipe into his pocket and stood.

122

The old man angled his walking stick ahead of him and stepped slowly down the hill. The collie circled the old man as he descended. The dog avoided crushing the dancing dandelions in the light breeze.

Every morning and evening in the winter months, Malachy's son arrived on his mountain bike, wearing a loose raincoat, a woolly cap, wellingtons and blue jeans. The old man would sometimes be around the cow house or out at the beech tree, lighting his pipe. One day, the old man was on his hunkers, at the back of the cubicle house. When he heard the bicycle, the old man surprised himself at the speed he was able to stand and fix his trousers, then walk around to the cow house, the walking stick in front, the collie circling him. The cow house was obsolete, it held no cow and had not done for many years, even though the cow milking number was still over the door.

The cow house held bales of hay when there was no room in the hayshed. The cow house also held many of the old man's tools which he had used for building, including his bricklaying trowel, his shovel, his handsaw, his chisel, his lump hammer, his claw hammer, his measuring tape, his building line, his bucket of nails, his straight edge, his hand plane  and spirit level, his plastering hawk and plastering trowel. There was also a petrol cement mixer Malachy had bought to fill the foundations of his bungalow. The last cow in the cow house had died on the farm early in Malachy's married life. Malachy's wife then bought milk with the rest of her weekly shopping in the new supermarket in town in the 1980s. The milk from the supermarket was pasteurized. It tasted different. Malachy's wife did not go to the travelling shop as the old man's wife did every Friday morning at eleven. The old man's wife wore a headscarf and walked down the boreen when the travelling shop came, carrying a wicker basket and a sheet of paper with items written in pencil.  She bought soda bread and apple pie and bacon and cabbage and potatoes and sugar and butter and washing powder and sometimes, rarely, salt, and many other items now that she did not bake, nor rear hens or pigs, nor grow and cultivate and harvest garden fruit and vegetables, not now, not anymore. At the back of the travelling shop, the man known as Eamon would open the double doors. Eamon always wore a long white coat and a pair of spectacles and he had a pencil behind his ear, with which he would tot up the bill in a little book when the old man's wife had ordered all of her weekly shopping. 'Good Morning, Mrs McNee,' Eamon would say to the old man's wife every week. The old man's wife also always bought a Lucozade in an orange bottle wrapped in golden cellophane which she placed on a newspapered shelf at the bottom of the sideboard until Malachy's son came to visit for tea and marmalade sandwiches. The old man's wife always went to the travelling shop alone. The old man did not know about his wife also buying the Lucozade. If he did, he would not have had any opinion on it. Malachy's wife went to the new supermarket in town on Thursdays and arrived back at the house with a car boot full of plastic bags of good things. Malachy's son helped his mother put away all of the shopping, enjoying a slice of turkey roll and coleslaw as he put everything into all of the presses in the kitchen.

When Malachy's son arrived every day in the winter, he took a bag of calf nuts from the cow house out of a blue barrel. He used a small blade to open the bag at the top. Then he carried the bag into the yard, by the cubicle house. He climbed the gate and poured the bag quickly into the steel trough, stamping through the muck, trying to avoid getting knocked over by the racing cattle, as they craved the sweet nuts, formed from the bones of their ascendants. Then he would cut the silage at the pit and grape six barrows into the three half-moon feeders. The new concrete trough that

Malachy had decided to build would make this job a little easier.

The old man stopped in the yard by the stack of blocks and the small pile of sand. There were some bags of cement covered with a plastic sheet on a wooden pallet. The old man leaned on his stick. He was tired after the walk down the hill. He looked at his watch. It was almost half past nine. He looked across at Malachy's house. All the curtains were drawn. Malachy had never been good at keeping accurate time. The old man had always found that early was easy. But he knew that Malachy had distractions. The old man walked up and down the trench that Malachy had dug some weeks before. The collie sniffed the clay. The old man looked up to the apex of the cubicle house, where the starling chirped. It had squeezed another twig onto the muck. The starling fitted the twig further into place with its beak. The old man tapped his stick. He went across to the tractor parked in the hayshed. There was no key in the ignition. He pushed in the stopper. He went around to the small steel toolbox attached to one of the steering rods. He took out a spanner from the box. He joined two wires connected to the electric ignition. The tractor jerked. He went to the cab and moved the gear handle to the neutral position. Then he went back to the engine and touched the two wires together. The engine turned. After twenty turns, it ignited. A gust of grey smoke rose from the tall exhaust pipe. The collie barked and wagged its tail. The old man climbed into the tractor. The collie jumped into the cab and curled up behind the clutch pedal on the left. The old man had not driven the tractor, or any vehicle, for some years.

The old man had never been a good driver of mechanically propelled vehicles. He had bought a brand-new Morris Minor when he was forty years old and he had immediately crashed it into the forecourt wall of Paddy Reilly's new shop. He had repaired the car himself. He had repaired all the damaged wing. He also had to repair Paddy Reilly's forecourt. Soon after, he had driven the car into the garden wall of Donald's house. He repaired the car again. He repaired Donald's front wall. He then used the car only on very rare occasions, such as going to Mass or to a funeral where he always drove the car extremely slowly. He always held the steering wheel at the very base with his finger and thumb. He now slowly lifted the clutch in the tractor. The engine heaved. The transport box attached to the back of the tractor was caught in the ground. The old man reached for the lift lever and pulled it. The transport box rose. Then he let the clutch up and the tractor reversed. The collie sat up, watching the motion. The old man hit the stone wall behind and knocked over stones. He faced the tractor to the road. He put the gear handle into second, the gearbox roared with friction until the clutch was firmly pushed. He let up the clutch, the tractor jerked up the slight hill by the cow house, and the beech tree, and straight onto the road, where an oncoming car swerved to avoid the tractor. The driver looked back and saluted the old man. The old man did not respond. The front wheel ran against Paddy Reilly's forecourt wall but did not knock it. The old man reversed slowly. Then he drove in third gear to the quarry. The steering wheel jerked as the old man turned in the open gate of the quarry. He backed the transport box to the small pile of chippings. He reversed into the chippings. The transport box filled. He lifted the box. The collie jumped out at the noise of scraping stones, circled the tractor, barked. The old man got out, taking the shovel from the cab. He spooned more gravel into the box. He kept going until the box was full.

The old man sprinkled salt on his plate. His wife sat by the range, with her legs crossed. She scratched her chin and said,'18,19,20.' The old man cut a slice of bacon. He put a spoon of butter on the peeled potatoes and it melted. He took up a forkful of the cabbage. He put it in his mouth and chewed. The collie sat by the range, its head rested on its white paws. Its eyes were almost closed. The old man looked out the window, over the quarry, to the cubicle house and the hill with the dandelions dancing in the breeze.

'Did Malachy come?' the old man's wife said.

'No.'

'Oorah. I saw Mike pass.'

The old man's wife had not used the phrase 'Oorah,' when they had first met. She had not used it when they got married, not for many years. After she had turned approximately sixty, the old man noticed she had started using the expression 'Oorah,' perhaps, he thought instead of 'Oh.' But he could not be certain. 'I didn't see him.'

The collie looked up and then rested its head back on its paws.

The old man enjoyed his meal. When he was finished, he got up and went outside. The collie followed him. The old man's wife got up and washed the plate and the knife and the fork in the Belfast sink in the small back kitchen.

The old man walked down the road toward the cubicle house. Across the road from the beech tree, Paddy Reilly leant against the wall of his forecourt. The shop door was open. The shelves within were full of good things. Paddy Reilly turned as the old man neared.

'Hello Malcolm.'

'Hello Paddy.'

'Grand day.'

'Aye.'

In the cow house, the old man took his handsaw, his claw hammer, his spirit level, his measure tape and his bucket of nails. In the yard, he looked across to Malachy's house. The Volkswagen Golf was gone. The curtains had been drawn. The old man took the shovel and spread the base of the trench with the chippings from the transport box. The collie circled the work, panting. The old man flattened the base with a short piece of wood. Then he put the spirit level on the wood and checked the half-moon glass which showed a bubble. He scraped the stones, until the level rested the bubble between the two black lines.

The old man took a long length of wood and placed it on the top of the levelled stones. He marked the end of it with his pencil. He put the end of the handsaw against the edge of the wood, where the mark was, and drew a pencil line. He then drew another line along the top. He sawed off the end of the timber. He did not push the saw. He drew the blade lightly and it ran up and down in a smooth motion. Sawdust spilled on the concrete. The collie sniffed it and then circled the yard. The starling chirped overhead.

The old man cut a second piece the same length as the first. He placed these on top of the leveled stones. He measured across at the end and cut two further pieces. He took out his hammer and some six-inch nails from the bucket. He attached the four pieces of wood together. Then he placed the frame over the stones. He measured the distance from each corner. He tapped the ends of the frame until each corner to corner measurement was the same. He fixed the frame in place with chippings shoveled along the outside. He adjusted the top of the frame with the hammer, until the spirit level showed a bubble between the two black lines in the half-moon window on top. He checked corner to corner of the frame again for square.

The old man was tired now. He looked at his watch. It was after three o' clock. The old man sat on the concrete blocks and reached for his pipe. The collie settled by him on the concrete, resting its jaw on its white paws. Its eyes were almost closed. The old man put the stem of his pipe in his mouth and cupped the match box in the palm of his left hand, with the match held in his thumb and finger of his right, and he struck the match head against the side of the box, where the head exploded into a flame. He touched the flame onto the centre of the pot of the pipe and tiny coals glowed red. Grey smoke billowed into the air. Paddy Reilly had gone back into his shop and shut the door. The windows of the shop were boarded-up.

At half three, Malachy's car drove in the drive to the front of the bungalow. The old man could hear raised voices as Malachy and his wife went into the house. The old man put the smouldering pipe in his jacket pocket. He turned and walked to the cow house. He pulled the petrol cement mixer out and dragged it around by the cow house, past the hayshed and up to the yard. He opened the choke and pulled the starter cord. After a few attempts, the mixer started. He shut the choke. He filled a bucket of water from the drinking trough and poured it into the drum. Then he shoveled some of the chippings in. He split a bag of cement in two. He grunted as he lifted the half bag of cement into the drum. Cement blew into his face as he tipped the powder. The mixer turned and turned about.

It took two wheelbarrows of concrete to fill the wooden frame. The old man used a short piece of wood to scrape off the edges. He tapped the concrete until the surface was as smooth as glass.

The old man put two stones from the wall into the mixer drum with a bucket of water. The stones thumped gently against the drum as the old man washed the shovel, level and the timber straight edge.

The collie sniffed the fresh concrete. It lifted its paw.

'Get away!' the old man said. The collie whined and crossed the yard, its tail down. It went to the mixer now and barked and looked up at the turning drum and barked again, the tail now wagging high.

At five o'clock, the old man lifted his egg and put a pinch of salt into the eggcup. He put the egg back and then tapped the

129

shell. He lifted the cap and spooned out the white and yolk. The old man put strips of bread and sugar into his mug. He pushed it around for a few moments. He drank tea, ate the pog from the mug, and chewed soda bread from Eamon's travelling shop. The soda bread was not as good as the bread the old man's wife once made. But the old man's wife did not bake, not now, not anymore.

'Did Malachy come?' the old man's wife said, as she sat by the range with her legs crossed, her boots in the air, she scratched her chin.

'No,' the old man said.

After the old man had eaten, he sat on the other side of the range, by the two-bar heater, which he plugged into the wall. The collie curled up in front of the range. The old man put the stem of his pipe into his mouth and lit the pot with a match. There was no need to cup his hands inside. The smoke rose toward the timbered ceiling as the tiny coals glowed red. A tractor passed on the road and turned up the boreen, passing the old man's house.

'That's Mike down again,' the old man's wife said, as she brought the eggcup, plate, teacup, mug, and cutlery out to the back kitchen where she would wash them in the Belfast sink. When she came back, she pushed a plug into the wall at the side of the window. The television on the other side of the room came on. An advertisement for a new car filled the screen. When the Angelus began, a picture of Our Lady in a stained-glass window replaced the advertisements. A sound of bell ringing came. The old man's wife stood and began to pray with her hands together. The old man did not pray aloud. The news came on after the Angelus. The old man's wife sat. When the news was over, the old man's wife pulled the plug out of the wall and the television screen went blank.

The old man waited on the hill. Across his line of vision, at the apex of the cubicle house roof, he watched the starling push in the rougher corners of the nest, until it was evenly sloped down to a pointed end. The nest was complete. The old man could see moss in the crevices of the galvanized sheeting. The dandelions danced in the invisible breeze. The old man scarchcd in his jacket pocket and pulled out his pipe. He put the stem in his mouth and lit the pot in the same fashion as he always did. The tiny coals glowed red. The old man coughed. Smoke billowed into the air. The collie looked up and sniffed. Swallows moved *en masse* through the leaves of the beech tree. Through the grey cloud of smoke, the old man could see the white of the swallow's breast as it stopped on a branch and scanned the yard. The swallow chirped. The old man wondered then, what, if any, kind of musical instrument could ever make the same sound as the swallow singing. The collie flicked its tail. The old man looked down the hill to the cubicle house, to the dungstead on the left, and on to the quarry. Further on, at his house, on the corner of the boreen, smoke unfurled from one of the decorative chimney pots on the roof. The other decorative chimney pot was not used, not now, not anymore. The old man's wife had lit the range early in the morning. She sat now beside the Stanley, under the large wooden mantlepiece with a design of Xs and zigzag lines and half-moons and little squares in diagonal lines. On the top there were two porcelain brown dogs at each end. In between were many other items, including fly killer spray, a calendar, a nail clippers and a large box of matches. Other items were taken and removed by the old man's wife. But the two porcelain dogs had never been moved since they had been placed there. The old man's wife sat in her usual chair with her legs crossed. She scratched her chin and counted aloud: '18,19,20'. It was twenty past nine on the old man's watch. He looked over to Malachy's house. All the curtains were drawn. The old man got up off the flat stone and used his walking stick ahead of him as he descended from the hill, the collie circling him all the time, the old man prodding the grass with his walking stick, avoiding the dancing dandelions. A dog howled in the distance as they reached the yard. The collie growled.

'Be quiet!' the old man said. A breeze drew a rattling noise from the galvanized roof of the cubicle house.

The old man walked up and down the foundations. He could smell the fresh concrete. He looked across to Malachy's house. The curtains were drawn. The Volkswagen Golf was parked in the drive. The boy's mountain bike was by the back door. The old man went across the yard, by the hayshed and into the path by the cow house. In the cow house, he took his claw hammer, his pinch bar, his bucket holding his bricklayer's trowel, his building line, his lump hammer and his bolster. He brought these into the yard. With the shovel, he drew back all the supporting chippings around the timber frame, until it was completely exposed. He applied the pinch bar with the claw hammer and tapped until each section of frame loosened and came off the concrete. The foundations had set very well. The old man was happy to see the form. He put the pinch bar back into the cow house. He took the bricklayer's trowel, the orange building line, the lump hammer, and the spirit level with the yellow bucket. In the yard the old man started the mixer. He poured in a bucket of water, then shoveled in sand with half a bag of cement. He watched it mix. He put blocks into the wheelbarrow and wheeled them over to the foundation. He came back to the mixer and tipped the mortar into the barrow and brought it over to the foundation. He turned the mixer off. The old man was tired now. He looked at his watch. It was after ten o'clock. He looked over to Malachy's house. The curtains were still drawn. He sat on the remaining blocks and reached for his pipe. The collie curled up by the old man's boots and lifted his tail gently before letting it rest again. The old man took out his pipe and put the stem into his mouth. He took out his matches.

He held the box in the palm of his left hand and held the match in the thumb and index finger of his right, cupping his fingers around it as he struck the match head on the side of the box. The flame exploded and he put it to the coals in the pot of the pipe. The coals glowed red. Smoke drifted up from the old man. A tractor started. The old man could not see very far from where he sat now in the yard, but he knew it was Mike's Massey Ferguson 135 that he could hear. He listened to it drive along the boreen, by the remains of Donald's house, stopping by the junction at the old man's house. Then Mike drove up by the quarry. As Mike's tractor passed by the beech tree, Mike looked into the yard. He saluted the old man. But the old man did not respond. The old man watched Mike turn at Malachy's house and drive down the road, revving the engine more now as it passed The Laughing Horse Inn and Yates' Well. The old man got up and walked across to the foundations, the collie up and circling him, tail in the air. The old man took the bricklayer's trowel from the bucket. He troweled some mortar onto one end of the foundation. He took a block and squeezed it down, leaving a half-inch bed, and eyeing it so it was parallel with the line of the foundation frame. He put the spirit level on top of the block and tapped the block with the lump hammer until the bubble in the half moon glass on top of the level was between the two black lines. Then the old man turned the spirit level the other way and tapped the block again until the spirit level was true. He then put the level adjacent to the side of the block and plumbed until the bubble in the circular window at the top of the level was between the two black lines. Now the block was in the correct position. The old man went to the other end of the foundation. He set another block in the same way as the first. He then took the building line from the bucket, hooked the nail into a loop at the end and pushed the nail into the bed of soft mortar under the second block. He unrolled the line around the block, brought it to the top edge and then drew the line down to the first block, wrapping it around this block in the same way and securing it around a loose block in the yard. Now the line was in position. The old man eyed the line at each end to make sure the two blocks were perfectly in line, tapping one corner with his bricklayer's trowel. The old man then troweled mortar all along the building line. He laid a line of blocks on this mortar, troweling mortar onto each end of every block as he laid it. When he got to the end, the space was shorter than a full block. He measured the gap. He measured the same distance on another block. He drew a pencil line along the smooth edge of the saw blade. He then applied the bolster to this line. He tapped the bolster with the lump hammer until the block split. He fitted the cut block in the remaining space and filled the mortar into the joint with the trowel. He tidied up all the joints now with extra mortar. The old man was tired. He sat on the remaining blocks and lit his pipe. It was after eleven o'clock. He looked across to Malachy's house. The starling chirped over the old man's head. As he looked up to the nest, he could see the little grey head of the bird moving. The collie sat beside the old man, his jaw resting on his white paws, his tail twitched gently, his eyes slowly closing.

The old man sprinkled salt over his plate. The old man's wife sat by the Stanley range, her legs crossed, her boots in the air. She scratched her chin and counted '18,19,20'. The old man cut a slice of bacon and put a knob of butter on the potatoes as he peeled each one. He took up a forkful of cabbage, put it in his mouth and chewed. He looked out the window, down across the quarry, to the cubicle house, the beech tree, Malachy's house under the hill.

　　'Mike went by,' the old man's wife said.
　　'I didn't see him,' the old man said.

Malachy's car was gone from the front of the house when the old man came back to the yard. He put his pipe in his mouth. The collie sniffed the line of blocks. The old man mixed the mortar with the trowel for some moments, adding a drop of water until it was again soft. Then he troweled out another line by the first line of blocks. The collie wagged its tail and circled the yard. The starling chirped from its new nest. The old man wondered again if any musical instrument could make the same sound, this time thinking of the starling instead of the sparrow. He laid the next line of blocks on their wide face. He worked quickly as the first line of blocks guided him. Yet he checked the blocks were level on their surface. Swallows rose *en masse* from the beech tree. Cattle groaned in the fields behind the hill. The old man then built a third line by the second, these on their edge, as the first line were, while the sun moved toward the east. But the old man knew it was not the sun that moved. He closed each end of the trough with a single block. He tidied all the joints once more. He put stones and a bucket of water into the mixer. As the drum turned, the stones banging the side of the drum, some of the water splashing out, the sound echoing around the yard, the old man washed the trowel and the shovel. The old man went to the mixer and tipped the water and stones out into the yard. The stones bounced on the concrete, now rounder and smaller than when they had been thrown in. The water rolled slowly toward the dungstead, some of it stopping in the corner of the slab and fading into the concrete. The drum was clean and shone a sparkling grey. The old man threw a bucket of water over the outside, scrubbing it with the yard brush.

'Now, do you see?' the old man said to the collie.

A car entered Malachy's driveway. The old man looked across. Malachy got out of the Golf and went into the house.

135

At five o'clock, the old man lifted his egg and put a pinch of salt into the egg cup. He put the egg back and then tapped the shell. He lifted the cap and spooned out the white and yolk. The collie was curled up under the table. The old man put strips of bread and sugar into his mug. He pushed it around for a few moments. He drank tea, ate the pog from the mug, and chewed soda bread from Eamon's travelling shop.

'Did Malachy come?' the old man's wife said, as she sat by the range with her legs crossed, her boots in the air, she scratched her chin.

'No,' the old man said.

Afterward, he sat on the other side of the range, by the two-bar heater, which he plugged into the wall. The collie curled up in front of the range. The old man's wife took the eggcup, plate, teacup, mug and cutlery and washed them all in the Belfast sink in the back kitchen. The old man lit his pipe. There was no need to cup the match and box inside. The flame made the coals in the pipe glow red. The collie curled in front of the Stanley range. The old man turned on the two-bar heater. A tractor slowed on the main road and turned down the boreen.

'That's Mike now,' the old man's wife said as she came back into the kitchen. She put a plug into a socket beside the window. The television at the other end of the room came on. An advertisement for a perfume filled the screen. When the Angelus bell sounded, the screen was filled with a stain glass window with an image of Jesus Christ. A sound of bell ringing came. The old man's wife stood in front of the Stanley range and prayed. The old man did not pray aloud. After the Angelus was over, the news came on. The old man's wife sat by the range. When the news was over, the old man's wife pulled the plug out of the wall and the screen went blank.

The old man waited on the hill. The starling was perched still in the nest in the apex of the cubicle house roof. Dandelions on the hill danced in the morning breeze. The collie sat by the old man's boots, its eyes half-open. The old man took his pipe from his jacket pocket, put the stem in his mouth. He lit the pipe with a match held in his thumb and index finger, his left hand holding the box in his palm. The remaining fingers shielded the flickering flame from the breeze for the second before it lit the tiny coals in the pipe pot. But the tobacco within was done. The old man tossed away the spent match. He tapped the pipe against the stone. The collie looked up at the noise. The old man inspected the pot. He tapped it again. He reached in his jacket pocket and took out a plastic pouch with 'Old Holborn' stamped across the front. He put pinches of the tobacco into the pot, pressing it down firmly as he did. When he had the pot filled, he put the pouch away. He lit the pipe in the same fashion. The freshly lit tobacco smoke was grey and silver and rose in plumes to the air. The old man drew the smoke deep into his lungs, the little coals glowed red. It was a quarter to nine on the old man's watch. All curtains were still pulled in Malachy's house. The Volkswagen Golf was in the drive. The old man got up slowly and went down the hill, prodding the grass with his walking stick. The collie circled him, the pink tongue hanging out, white paws soft against the dirt. A breeze whistled through the leaves of the beech tree, rattling the galvanized sheets of the cubicle house roof.

In the cow house, the old man found the plastering trowel and hawk, the aluminum straight edge and the wooden float. He put these tools with the bucket and a sponge into the wheelbarrow and wheeled it to the yard. The old man was tired. He looked at his watch. It was twenty past nine. He sat on the remaining blocks and reached into his jacket pocket for his pipe. In one of Malachy's windows, the curtains were being drawn. The old man checked the pot of his pipe. He put the stem of the pipe in his mouth. A door opened, the back door of Malachy's house. Malachy's son came out and walked by the mountain bike, out the drive. The old man watched him cross the road, walk across to Paddy Reilly's forecourt and enter the shop. A few moments later, the boy came out with two cartons of milk. He walked across the road and in the drive and into Malachy's house. The old man lit his pipe. The coals in the pot glowed red. The starling chirped overhead. At almost ten o'clock, Malachy and his son came out of the house. They got into the Volkswagen Golf. Malachy drove out the drive, down the road by Paddy Reilly's shop and stopped by the beech tree, parking outside the cow house. Malachy and his son got out.

Malachy was speaking as he got out of the car. He pointed across the road to Paddy Reilly's shop. 'It's just rotting away there. I don't see what the family will do with it. Probably sell the whole thing.'

'Well,' Malachy said to the old man as they came into the yard.

'Well,' the old man said.

'What the bleddy hell?' Malachy stopped and looked at the built trough. 'You have it built! And you even put in a bleddy foundation! Why did you bother with that?'

'Keep it from cracking. Calves pushing against it.'

'Ah! No need, no need. It was only an old trough. Granda has it built, Malcolm. But we can plaster it now. Get the mixer going, look lively!' Malachy said.

It seemed then there were many shovels, buckets and people in the yard. The old man smoked as he sat on the blocks. Malachy and his son filled the mixer with sand, cement and water.

When the mix was ready, Malachy's son tipped the mortar into the wheelbarrow and wheeled it over to the trough. He tipped it onto a sheet of plywood that Malachy had placed there. Then the son returned to the mixer and started to fill it again. Malachy knelt at one end of the trough. He held the hawk in his left hand and the trowel in his right.

'Leave that mixing away and come over here, Malcolm!' Malachy said. The son came across. 'Shovel muck onto the hawk now.' The boy tipped a shovel of mortar onto the hawk Malachy held up.

Malachy grunted under the weight, then lifted a trowelful off the hawk in a quick movement and spread the mortar across the blocks. After Malachy had most of the first side of the trough coated, the old man got up and walked across the yard. He took up the straight edge and dipped it in the water trough. 'No need for straightening,' Malachy said. 'We'll float it up rough, sure it's only an old trough.' But the old man applied the straight edge to the plaster, scraping off lumps, tossing the excess into the barrow. With a short piece of wood, the old man filled the hollows and drew the straight edge over the plaster again, until the plaster was flat. Malachy went to the other side and coated the blocks.

The old man continued to smoothen the plaster with the straight edge and the piece of wood.

After the trough was plastered inside and out, Malachy ordered the son to wash out the mixer with stones and water. Malachy began to rub the plaster with the wooden float, until it became sealed and smooth. The noise of the mixer rattling echoed around the yard.

'Do you want to try a bit of floating, Malcolm?' Malachy said to the son.

The boy came across and took the wooden float. He started to rub some of the plaster not yet floated. Bits of the plaster came off the blocks. 'Not like that, not like that! Watch what you're doing! Gently!' Malachy said. 'Lighter.' The boy lightened the pressure he applied to the float and the plaster came smooth.

The old man left the yard and walked up the hill, prodding the grass with his walking stick, the collie circling him, nosing the ground, the tail wagging high, the dandelions dancing in the soft morning breeze. At the flat stone, the old man turned and sat, watching the floating of the trough below, the noise of smooth wood on wet plaster echoing around the yard. He reached for his pipe. He coughed and then lit the tobacco in the pot in the usual fashion. Smoke lifted. The collie curled by the old man's boots.

The boy had knocked more mortar off the blocks.

'You have to be more careful, do you hear me?' Malachy said, his voice rising up the hill to the old man. 'Rome wasn't built in the one day.' Malachy went to the holes and filled them with mortar using his hawk and trowel. The boy pushed the float again, too hard and the plaster fell off the wall.

'No, no, no! You're not listening to me at all! Give me the bleddy float! And gather up them cement bags and burn them!'

The boy put the float in the barrow and went across to the sand, where he gathered all the empty cement bags.

Malachy completed floating all the plaster on the trough, inside and outside. The old man watched Malachy square up the inside corners of the trough with the trowel. Malachy tidied up the external corners and edges by floating the plaster into a straight piece of timber and then carefully sliding it away. Then he half-filled the bucket with water from the water trough. He dipped the sponge. He went with the bucket and sponge to the plaster. He rubbed the sponge over the plaster. It became fine. Although the old man could not see from his flat stone, he knew that the tiny sand stones were coming shiny and clean to the surface.

The boy looked up the hill. The old man sat still on the flat stone. The boy took out a lighter and lit one of the bags, cupping the flame with his fingers, using his body to shield the

140

flame from the breeze. He turned the lit bag inwards to protect the flame and lay it in the corner of the yard. He put the rest of the cement bags over the first bag. Smoke rose in plumes. The bags caught fire. The boy looked up again to the hill. The old man was silhoucttcd against the sunlight. The boy looked beyond, charred paper rose with the smoke toward the sky, where another plane passed, a tiny white dot leaving a silver line in its wake.

II

Malcolm stood by the beech tree. There was a crowd of people standing in the field at the foot of the hill. A man wearing a suit of tweed, a white shirt and a blue tie stood on the flat stone at the top of the hill. He turned the pages of a little black book. He had a shock of red hair under his hat. Now he put the book away and looked at the people below.

'Good afternoon, gentlemen,' the man said, his voice echoing down the hill to the roadside. 'I am Henry P. Cooke of Cooke Auctioneers and Valuers, authorized in the licensing and sale of premises and lands and registered with the District Court as a Commissioner of Oaths. Good day to one and all. Good to be with you gentlemen on this fine spring morning.'

Malcolm looked down to the quarry, where two men filled a cart with stones, the sound echoing around the crater and up the auction site by the beech tree. Cooke coughed.

'Now lads, as ye all know only too well, only too well, this fine parcel of land is the premium lot on the market around here for some miles, as I can see by the large crowd here today. And not only that, gentlemen, but it comes with the bonus of what I may say is  a fantastic, elevated site, overlooking the entire village,' Cooke raised and stretched his left arm, 'a piece of land adjacent to the world famous The Laughing Horse pub, a 17$^{th}$ century Inn, just a few hundred yards across the way.' Cooke pointed behind the crowd, 'And this site is right across from the post office, ran by the very respectable Mr Patrick Reilly Esquire, who I can see is in the attendance today, welcome Paddy. Now, just take a look, gentlemen, if you will, at the wonderful view from here.'

Cooke panned his left arm as he spoke, over the village, beyond the quarry to the left, the site-under-construction at the corner of the boreen, where lines of shuttered walls stood. The crowd followed his arm, even though they were all familiar with the terrain, it had never been pointed out to them in just this way.

'And here to my right, poor Mr Kennedy's old home, which has sadly fallen into disrepair these past few years. But this site can of course be indeed reborn by some talented young saw-and-chisel of which I am sure there are some amongst you. Now that's not all, gentlemen. Oh no! This particular lot also includes twenty acres of the finest arable land, appropriate for very minor stock reproofing.' Cooke nodded casually toward a line of rotting fenceposts amongst the hawthorn bushes. 'And suitable for all types of beef and sheep farming, and with a little reconditioning, even fine tillage. As you all no doubt know, the farm is accessible from all sides, surrounded as it is by the roads around this fair village. So, it really does have the potential to be a very sound investment. It will quickly repay your hard-earned notes, year after year, for a lifetime and even many lifetimes. Oh yes, a wonderful, fantastic, great opportunity to acquire a monumental piece of real estate, or my name is not Henry P. Cooke Esquire of Cooke Auctioneers and Valuers and Registered Commissioners for Oaths with the District Court!'

'Sure how do we know it is?' someone shouted. There was laughter.

'Ho ho! Glad to see the old humour for which this area is famous for!'

There were further comments and laughter. Mike Feerick and Paddy Reilly stood at the foot of the hill, looking up at Cooke. Malcolm knew these were the only two serious contenders for the Kennedy farm. It had been well discussed in the Horse that Reilly wanted to build a new shop on the site of Kennedy's house, moving the post office in with it. Mike wanted to double his farm by joining the road locked parcel onto his. Both were said to have the notes. Donald Watt was the only other possible farmer who could have an interest locally. But he had already sold land to Mike Feerick. Watt had no sons to farm for. He had only two daughters. One had emigrated and was settled in England. The other had married a young carpenter, whose father was a builder. That family were said to know nothing of farming. Watt had hired his son-in-law's family to build a new house for him at the end of the boreen with the money he got for land, but he was said to have stretched himself too far with it. He was said to be cleaned out once it was completed. It had cost more than he had expected, but he had to finish it, or he would be a complete disgrace in the village. The only serious contenders were Mike Feerick and Paddy Reilly. Yet the entire village of farmers had attended the auction, except for Watt, who, the village knew, now spent most of the day in his bed, as he suffered a lot from 'The Nerves'.

'Poor Johnny Kennedy will farm no more,' Cooke was saying, 'but you can continue the honest work he was doing all his life. Yes, that's right, I am talking to one of you astute gentlemen. The family in England that looked after poor Johnny's affairs these last few years are happy to let the place go to a keen farmer at a very, very reasonable price. And I am sure it is a sorry sight for the village to see the centerpiece of their homeland go so neglected. But the lucky purchaser will be able to put it right. And of course, he will not just get twenty acres of the finest arable land and a premium house site! Oh no! He will also acquire a very rich limestone quarry, with plenty of mileage left in her! Yes, that's over there to your right, gentleman!' Cooke stretched his left arm and the

143

villagers, who had all passed the quarry many thousands of times, still turned to look at it with fresh eyes. Two men continued shoveling stones into their cart, the ass looking, not at the auction, but docilely ahead.

'Kennedy's quarry has supplied Malachy McNee & Son Builders for twenty years and provided the mass concrete walls of many state scheme houses around this region. Mr McNee once told me in the Horse that finer limestone for building could hardly be got anywhere. I suppose you could say I got that information straight from the Horse's mouth!' Weak laughter rose.

'Mr McNee also said that, in his opinion as a user of the quarry for two decades, there was yet enough stone there for the rest of the century. As no one here will see the end of this or any other century, I'd put it to ye wise gentleman that'd be a nice additional lifetime side income from this opportunity!'

Cooke looked to the beech tree. 'And as good fortune would have it, I see Mr McNee's son, Malcolm, is with us today, over there by the beech tree!'

Everyone turned instantly and looked at Malcolm. 'I see you are harvesting some right as we speak down there! Leave a little for the new man now!' There was further laughter. 'Am I right about that stone, Malcolm?'

'It's good stone alright.'

'Well, well, well. Now what more do ye men want? I'm sure a starting price of £2,500 is more than reasonable!'

Malcolm got on his bicycle. He cycled down the road, away from the auction, to the quarry. Padraig and Tom stopped shoveling the stones as he cycled in. Malcolm took the third shovel and began filling the cart.

'Well, Malcolm. Who got it?' Padraig said.

'No one yet, it's just started.'

'What are you doing down here?'

'I'm out.'

144

'Why that?'

'Two and a half grand, that's the why.'

'Ah! That's only the starting price.'

'You should whip it,' Tom said.

'Ye must think I'm rich.'

'Borrow it. I'd loan it to you if I had it. The stone in that quarry.'

'Aye. Worth millions if you could get it out.'

'Great chance, Malcolm.'

'That cart is full,' Malcolm said. Padraig started the jennet and they followed the cart out of the quarry. A boy of fifteen came along the road on a bicycle as they turned for Donald's site.

'Do you need a hand filling the shutters today, Malcolm?'

'It would be good, but I've only three shovels with me.'

'Is the auction done?' Padraig said.

The boy shrugged. 'It's in a stalemate. Nothing is happening the last while. It's got boring.' Malcolm looked up. Cooke sat on the flat stone, head in hands. Paddy Reilly had his fists against his hips. Mike was shaking his head.

'Why don't you go up and see, Malcolm?' Padraig said. 'That land might not be sold again for a hundred years. That's the thing about land. You never know when it will become available. I'm surprised auctioneers never make more of that.'

'They're salivating for the money, that's why, they haven't time to think. Aye, Padraig is right, go up there Malcolm, and give them a roasting!' Tom said. The men laughed. The boy took the third shovel from Malcolm.

Malcolm parked his bicycle at the beech tree. Cooke had stood again by the stone. He wiped his glasses with a large handkerchief.

At the foot of the hill. Paddy Reilly drew smoke from his pipe. Mike twisted a finger in his ear. Some of the villagers watched Cooke. The auctioneer spread out his arms.

'Lads!' Cooke shouted. 'This farm is at the centre of your fine village. It has the post office, the pub, the school, the church just over the road. It has everything a little village could want. Now look at the land, look at the site. Look at the quarry. This is a paradise. A paradise ye could let slip through yere fingers. Lost forever. One day this chance is here. The next it is gone.'

Cooke walked around in a circle and faced the villagers again. 'I ask ye, when will an opportunity like this come again? When? Maybe not for ten decades. That's the thing about land. You never know when it will come back on the market. Not maybe for a century. We'll be all well-rotted away by then. But this land. This land, gentlemen. This land lasts. Money loses its value. We all know that. We all know what a penny would have bought twenty years ago and what it'll buy now. Them pound notes ye have in the mattress. Every year they're worth less. They're weakening by the day. They're going damp, and rotten and risking mould the longer they are hidden there.' There was muttering and laughter in the crowd. 'But land is land. Now ye can't expect, in all fairness, a grieving family beyont in England to sell their uncle's farm, to sell off the inheritance of their children and their children's children and even beyond that for fifteen hundred pounds? Can ye? I'm surprised at men of yere ilk. I'd have expected men like ye to value land more that that. Surely ye all know good land when ye see it? The bidding has to pick up...' Cooke looked around the group before him. 'Have I any advance?' There was silence for some moments. Cooke sat on the flat stone and cupped his jaw.

146

Malcolm walked in by the villagers who now spoke in low tones. He passed Paddy Reilly and Mike Feerick. He climbed the hill to Cooke.

'Ah, young Mr McNee. You can tell your father I'll make sure to ask whoever buys it to give him the nod for the stone, don't worry. He was on to me about it already. If we ever sell it, that is.' Cooke spoke with little interest. 'I heard he was off work. Is he not well?''

'The Doctor told him to stay at home for a while and rest up.'

'Rest up, that's right. Leave it to the young spades like yourself.'

'What's the price?'

'The price? Ah, there's no price at the moment. I need at least eighteen hundred to even go on the market with this lot. These two...' Cooke nodded down the hill to Reilly and Mike. They both stared at the ground. 'They know that only too well.'

'Eighteen hundred? Is that how much they want?'

'They want a lot more than that. That's the base price.'

Malcolm looked down the hill. 'I'll give them eighteen hundred for it, Mr Cooke.'

'You will?'

'Aye.'

Cooke stared at Malcolm for a few moments. 'Right. Right, right, right. Well, we'll have to auction it. That's the law.'

'By all means.'

Malcolm walked down the hill. Cooke was back on the flat stone, standing by the time Malcolm got back to the beech tree.

Cooke clapped his hands. 'Gentlemen, it seems like a bit of sense has come around to the place at last. Now, I'm officially resuming the auction here, by the law vested in me

147

from the office of the District Court judge. I have a local bid on the table of eighteen hundred pounds.'

Everyone looked back at Malcolm.

'I'm authorized to go on the market with it, the lot will sell today. So...well, well, well! This is still a great price for such a holding. Do I have eighteen twenty?'

Paddy Reilly spat. He walked out to the edge of the road, looked back at Cooke and the quarry and passed Malcolm. He walked across to the post office. Mike had lit his pipe.

'Eighteen twenty, gentlemen? Eighteen twenty?'

Mike exhaled. He nodded at Cooke through the smoke.

'Thank you, Mike. Welcome back to the auction. And I see the Post Office has just reopened across the road.' There was loud laughter.

'Anyone else here for a bargain? Do I have eighteen fifty?'

Malcolm raised four fingers.

'Oh sorry, gentlemen. I thought we were dealing in manageable tranches. Apologies. Eighteen forty it is. Have I eight-six?'

Mike drew on his pipe. The coals glowed red.

'Lads,' Cooke stretched his arms as though to increase his height. 'It's a giveaway! Come on! Come on! Don't be bold with me!'

There were some mutterings amongst the villagers. Then silence fell. Mike walked back towards the beech tree. 'Hello Malcolm,' Mike said as he neared.

'Hello Mike.'

Mike stood close to Malcolm. Malcolm could hear the strains of Mike's breath. 'What are you spending today, Malcolm?'

'As it is, as it comes. Philomena is home. Did you see the motorcar?'

'I did, Malcolm. I did indeed.' Mike stood a little away.

Cooke dropped his shoulders. He jumped down off the stone. He stamped dandelions into the grass as he came down the hill. He grabbed a spade that had been stuck in the ground at the flat part of the field. He dug into the ground, grunting theatrically. He pulled up the scraw, dropping the spade, which clanged off a stone.

Cooke displayed the scraw to the villagers, panning in a semicircle.

'See that? The finest of fertile soil. The best this country, this island, has to offer. Imagine the cattle you could build up on that. Imagine the Easter lambs that could thrive on the ewe's milk from the rich, arable nutrients up out of that pure soil. Do ye think about that, do ye? Imagine the praties, carrots, cabbage, onions, fresh rhubarb you could reap on this patch?' Cooke stood still. 'By Jaysus, it's a slice of the Emerald Isle in God's Own County and no mistake! We have the Holy mountain pilgrims over the road  before us, the last Sunday of every July, where Paddy ran all the snakes out of your fair ground a thousand years ago, we have the blessed site of the  risen figures in our Chosen Town behind us, and now at the centre of it all we have the sacred plains of the county available at a giveaway price! Three miracles of nature!' Cooke sniffed the clay. 'Smell that earth!  Breathe it in! Now, I'm no farmer, but I reckon any manjack here today would pull two cuts of the sweetest hay from soil the like of that.'

Cooke placed the scraw gently back on the ground. He stamped back up the hill, crushing more dandelions as he did and stood again on the flat stone. 'Gentlemen, it's not the notes ye have stuffed under yere beds that makes men of ye. It's the fields around yere house that helps ye sleep better at night. That's what I'm talking about. We fought for the freedom of this land for the past nine hundred years!

149

And…blood and sweat spilt in…twenty wars! And now ye can have this place for a few hundred quid!'

Mike sucked on his pipe. Clouds drifted in front of Malcolm, he coughed. 'Right, gentlemen,' Cooke said. 'Let's get down to business. In my last contact with Mrs Bowles, I was authorized to put the parcel on the market once we get over £1800 – the lot will be sold today. Do I have £1860? Thank you, Mike, on the market now…at 1880? Thank you, Malcolm. Last chances, gentlemen. Have I nineteen hundred? I do. Return the ball. Nineteen twenty. Yes. Twenty, forty, forty, forty, forty, yes, on the money, six, six, six, sixty, sixty, return the ball, eight, eight, eight, eighty, eighty, yes, on the money, two thousand pounds, last chances…two thousand…don't be spitting, Mike!' Mike had stepped a few yards away from Malcolm. The crowd burst into laughter. 'What do you mean by that signal? Twenty twenty, is it? I said don't be spitting, but don't be splitting either!' The crowd laughed again. 'Twenty ten back to you, so, Malcolm. Don't be scowling at me, Mike!' The crowd laughed and looked back at Malcolm. 'Deadening at two thousand and ten pounds. The auction site went very quiet. In the distance, the three labourers emptied the cart onto a large board for mixing beside the shutters. Padraig placed a ladder against the walls to be filled. The sound of Tom filling a bucket of water from the barrel echoed up to the auction site. The young lad mixed more cement with chippings from the quarry. Tom poured water into the centre of the pile. 'Mike with twenty ten…are we all done at two thousand and ten pounds to Mike Feerick to acquire the Kennedy lot?'

Cooke looked down to the beech tree, to Malcolm. Malcom broke his gaze and looked beyond Cooke to the sky. The sun was stronger now and blinded him. He turned to the quarry through the sun rays. Over the quarry, he looked to the corner, to Donald's small fields, and the new house at the end of the boreen where Padraig went up the ladder with a bucket and poured concrete into the shutter as the others mixed on the board. Malcolm looked down the boreen to Donald's stone cottage, where Donald slept all day, every day. Further on he could see Mike's house. He looked left to Kennedy's fields and the derelict site. He could hear Reilly banging doors in the Post Office. Malcolm nodded.

'Two thousand and twenty to the young builder! But Mike! Where are you going, Mike!'

'Wether,' Mike said, as he took his bicycle from the ditch.

Laughter spread around the field. 'Twenty twenty…well, well, well! Are we all done then, two thousand and twenty pounds for the Kennedy farm to Mr Malcolm McNee…no late callers? Still a good price…no? One…two…Lot 43991 with Cooke Auctioneers & Valuers & Registered Commissioners for Oaths by the Local District Courts, sold to Mr Malcolm McNee! Congratulations, Malcolm!' The crowd applauded. Someone shook Malcolm's hand. Someone squeezed his shoulder. On the hill, Cooke wrote Malcolm's name in his black notebook. More villagers came to Malcolm, congratulated him.

Now Padraig took Malcolm's arm amongst the crowd gathered by the beech tree. 'Malcolm, Brendan is home from England. He's down at the quarry. He says it's your wife. She's taken bad.'

Malcolm cycled by the quarry and the site at the corner by the end of the boreen, where the others still mixed and filled the shutters. He cycled along the boreen to Donald's cottage. In the yard, there was a motorcar. Malcolm walked in by the asbestos roofed turf shed. He and Padraig had dug the foundations, but Donald had gotten another builder for the turf shed. Malcolm had a method for digging, shown to him by his father when he was a boy, a deft use of pick and spade. He cleared the foundation rapidly as Padraig filled the cart. Donald's daughter Rita had not emigrated with her sister Philomena. Rita wore a smart apron the sunny day that Malcolm and Padraig had been sent by Malcolm's father. Rita came with a silver teapot and rhubarb and apple pie covered with a tea cloth. She brought them two whiskeys in the evening. Malcolm asked Rita if she ever happened to go to the County Ballroom. It was a derelict landlord's house that had been converted into a large hall for dances. Rita had never heard of the event before. Malcolm arranged to come and collect her one evening.

Malcolm came into the kitchen. Donald's house had just three rooms and a wooden outhouse. He had asked Malcolm's father to build his new house at the end of the boreen, having fell out with the turfshed builder over money. Philomena got off Rita's chair by the large fireplace. She walked across and Malcolm noticed she was carrying a small bundle. 'This is your son, Malcolm. Congratulations.'

Malcolm took the baby, soft and smelling of carbolic soap and talcum powder. Brendan stood by the window.

'Congratulations, Malcolm!' He shook Malcolm's hand.

'He's from abroad. Europe.' Philomena said. 'But that doesn't matter now.'

'Rita is in the bedroom. We told her to wait in there until tomorrow anyway. In case of any callers.'

'Did ye have any trouble?'

'No trouble, Malcolm.'

'I'll go down to her.'

Malcolm carried the baby across the kitchen to the bedroom.

Rita sat on the side of the bed and looked up as Malcolm entered.

Malcolm linked Rita on the dancefloor of the County Ballroom. He had installed the floorboards with Tom and

Padraig. The music from the band on the high stage boomed. Rita twisted under Malcolm's arms. Malcolm was light and dazzling on his feet. Rita swung, her face a smile. It was like they floated, their steps and twists and turns gentle as they bumped into other dancers. Rita shouted, Malcolm laughed. Later, he would cycle back with her to Donald's house as the summer morning dawned. They would talk outside, he would kiss her by the freshly poured foundations of Donald's turfshed.

'You'd want to get under the blankets,' Malcolm said. 'For talk's sake.'

'It's the middle of the day.'

'What if someone comes? You can't be sitting there in your clothes. You're after giving birth.'

'Amn't I on the bed? Is that not enough for them?' Malcolm handed Rita the baby.

'Well. It's a boy anyway.'

'It'd want to be. There was enough women born under this roof.'

Rita held the baby in her arms. She pulled the blankets back and lay on the mattress, placing the baby on the pillow beside her.

'Take the bleddy boots off at least!'

'Leave me alone.'

Rita pulled the blankets up to her chin, the boots coming out at the end of the bed. Malcolm went down to the end of the bed and pulled Rita's boots off. Just the baby's face could be seen now on the pillow.

'He'll be a fine fellow.' Rita said.

'We better get him christened,' Malcolm said. 'And I bought Kennedy's place.'

'That'll do.'

Malcolm left the bedroom. In the kitchen, Philomena sat by the small fire. Brendan stood by the table at the window.

The baby cried. 'I thought she had him under control,' Brendan said and laughed.

Philomena went to the table and took up a wicker basket. 'He might need a drop of milk.' She went across to the bedroom.

Brendan sat on the chair by the fire. 'Well, I was furious I missed the auction. The ferry was delayed. I do enjoy Cooke's spin. He really should be in the circus, never mind handling people's land and money. Did Mike get Kennedy's in the end? I heard he was fighting with Paddy Reilly. Mike's wanted that quarry for years. The lads with the jennet said Reilly went off barking back to the post office.'

'I bought the place, Brendan. Two thousand and twenty.'

'You did? Good man! A son and a farm on the one day!'

'Aye.'

'You'll have Donald's house soon done. I imagine the four of you will fit there, it's a fine place judging by those shutters.' Brendan looked at the door behind him, to the left of the range. 'Lord knows Donald will hardly be in it with you too many years,' Brendan said in a lower voice. 'Let's have a drink. Has he still got that Jameson there in the sideboard?'

'Oh, he does.'

'What better time to drink it.'

Malcolm opened the press at the bottom of the sideboard. On a newspapered shelf, there was a bottle of Jameson whiskey. He took out two wrinkled glasses from the top and put them on the table. He poured them both to halfway. He handed one to Malcolm. They clinked glasses.

'Good luck!' They sipped the whiskey.

'It's a fine place, Malcolm, the Kennedy patch.  But that business with the family, those Bowles in England. It didn't do it any favours. The land will need a lot of work. And the old house Johnny had. But if anyone can turn it around,

154

you and your father can, once he gets back on his feet. It'd be a fine farm, there's no doubt. And that quarry. I'd say there's more than a few houses left in it. Could be a real goldmine. But don't listen to the spin. It won't make you a millionaire. If you can keep that contract your father has with the council, you'll have your own stone, so you should do very well. You'll get your pile together.'

Malcolm sat by the fire. 'Rita doesn't want me building at all. She wants me on Donald's farm. Anything to stop him selling off any more of it to Mike Feerick.' Malcolm finished his glass. He looked into the embers, two sods slowly burning, feeding off each other to send flames up toward the chimney, the glow tiny within the huge hearth. 'Farm, farm, farm. That's all I ever hear.'

'Ah. Did she ask Philomena?'

'Hie?'

Brendan took another drink. 'To give you a lift with Kennedys'?'

'No. I had twenty years of notes at home.'

'You're a very careful man.'

'I'm cleaned out now.'

'Still, that's good grazing, Malcolm.'

'The farm is twice the size. I'll have to call the building off altogether.'

'That's a shame. They say you're the best around.' The baby cried. 'Did she not get him milk?'

The door by the fireplace opened. Donald stood in long johns. 'Well.'

'Well, Donald.'

'Donald.'

'You got back from England alright?'

'There were a few gusts and the ferry was delayed. But we got here in the end. And we brought you a present.'

'A present?'

155

'A grandson. Congratulations.'

'I see.' Donald went to the table, his socks not fully on his feet. He took up the bottle. 'You are starting early.'

'It's a special day, Donald,' Brendan said. 'You may as well join us.'

'No thanks. Is there no nurse here? Even for talk's sake?

'We could get Sally Hughes? She's a mid-wife,' Malcolm said.

'That might draw more questions, Malcolm,' Brendan said. 'Questions with no answers. Best leave it alone would be my advice.'

'There's going to be a lot of talk around these boreens, that's all I know,' Donald said, and walked back to his bed.

Malcolm and Brendan returned from The Laughing Horse late in the night. Brendan was quite drunk. He tripped on the threshold and banged his head on the table. He wept in front of the fire and eventually fell asleep. Malcolm opened the bedroom door. Rita lay under the bedclothes, the baby beside her. Philomena slept under a blanket on the floor.

Malcolm walked outside, by the turfshed and down the boreen, the moon lighting up the two tracks of gravel either side of the grass. Malcolm stopped at the main road and walked in amongst the timber shutters. He walked through the wooden shapes, strange and white in the moonlight, the smell of fresh concrete and sawn timber rich in the air. He would strip the castings in two days. He would roof and plaster this house within the coming weeks. But it would, he knew, be his final contract. He would spend over a year getting Kennedy's farm put right. He would demolish the remains of Kennedy's old house. He would plough, rotavate and reseed all the fields for grazing. He would upgrade the fences. He would drain it and he would fill it with stock.

156

Without Malcolm, his father, in bad health, could not keep up with the work anymore. Malachy McNee had worked hard to get hold of the area deciding officer for the state scheme housing contracts years before, when the country became independent. Work like that did not come easy. There was always a list of builders snapping at the heels of the McNees. Toward the end of the following year, Malcolm's father died in his sleep. The state scheme contracts were grabbed by someone else with newer machinery. But it had already happened, Malcolm knew, as he rubbed his hand on a smooth timber joint. He walked out the site and down the boreen toward the little cottage on the corner, where he could see flashes of the dying fire hitting the glass of the window.

## III

The boy looked at the lines the Master had drawn under penciled numbers. He could not see any marks for mistakes on the page. He wondered if the whole page was a mistake.

He heard the front door of the Schoolhouse open.

'What took ya? Is that for scratching or bating, Reilly? Get over to that wall! Such a bunch of streeshing thicks I never did see! By Jaysus, ye'll learn yare sums tonight!'

The boy could hear whining. 'Shut it Feerick! There's a buachaill near half yare age in there can do the same tables. The whole class of ye should be ashamed!'

The boy looked over to the large hearth as the hawthorn whished through the air. He ran across to the fireplace. He took two sods from the bucket and put them on the red coals. Sparks rose to the chimney. There was a knock on the door. The whipping stopped. There were men's voices.

'Where are you going with a fire on a day of sun the like of this?' The boy turned around. His father stood in the doorway.

'We have to light one every day. No matter the weather. The Master said.'

'Don't mind what the Master said. You've no truck with the Master no more. Not from this day. Come on with me now. I need another body with a pick in Kennedy's quarry.'

Steel swung silver through the air, like a fan of falling hammerheads, onto the face of smooth, freshly sledge-split limestone, which became quickly marked and wrinkled and broken up into small pieces, with each impact of each pickaxe. Dust rose thick into the boy's face, eyes, nose, mouth, ears, his hair grew quickly white. He was winded. His little hands, soft from the pencil of the schoolhouse, gripped the large handle, became cut and bled, the pickaxe was half his length. The boy's legs wobbled and his chest heaved. The rest of the gang that worked alongside him were much taller and broader, they had stubble on their chins, rolled-up sleeves and turned-down wellingtons, the shouts of their exchanges boomed as they worked, smoke from their pipes and cigarettes mixed in the white lime dust, it seemed then to the boy that the others could swallow him whole if they wanted.

'Come on, come on, we only have the one day!' The boy's father walked up and down by the quarry gate, a collie trailing after him, smoke lifted from the chestnut pipe. Grey dusted yellow laced boots crunched the sunlit stones. 'The sky is falling in tomorrow!' The boy's throat was dry as he tried to swing the pick-axe as fast as the others. He began to think in the glaring sun of mugs and mugs of cold sparkling water from Yates' Well by The Laughing Horse, an ice-cold thirst-killing drink, he felt as if he was there with a mug, he would drink for hours and hours.

Johnny Kennedy was at the quarry gate. 'You'll have to get one of them big machines down from Dublin, Malachy. I hear they do some shifting,' Kennedy said to the boy's father.

158

'I have all the machines I want right here, Johnny. They run a lot cheaper than the Dublin chassis!'

They laughed. All of the pick-axes stopped. The boy stepped forward as most of the others did, some of the men stood behind, scooping up the loose stones into a cart. The pick-axes swung once more.

'That lad is a bit light yet for the pick, is he?' Kennedy said, looking at the boy.

'We just got him out of the school today. The hands are soft from the books. But he'll soon harden. He's alright. He'll not die,' the boy's father said.

'My young man is in bed with the flu.'

'The flu is in the weather, some type of it.'

'Aye, I don't know what these lads are coming to. Maybe you could give me that buckeen for a few hours. I'm putting on a little roof on a henhouse.'

'A course, Johnny. Malcolm! Malcolm!'

The boy stopped swinging the pick-axe and turned in a giant cloud of white dust.

'Mr Kennedy needs a hand with a roof. Go with him. Leave the pick-axe there.'

The boy put the pick-axe against the cart, now half-full with stones and he walked out by his father, through the quarry gate and down the road with Johnny Kennedy, the pick-axes and shovels and stones clanging and making scraping noises behind as they walked by a line of beech saplings and Reilly's farmhouse.

They stopped at the head of the road and turned in the gate to Kennedy's house. There was a neat garden lined with box hedge around the front and a stepped concrete path. The house was neatly thatched, with three rooms inside. A woman worked by the side wall, washing clothes in a large barrel.

'You got help,' the woman said.

'I have to, with Charlie useless,' Kennedy said. 'This is young McNee. Son of the builder.'

'Sure that boy is only about ten, Johnny. Is he not going to the Schoolhouse? Could you not have got an older lad?'

'They are mining the quarry today., His father picked him out so he must think he's ready for work. That's all I know about it.'

'Hello, young man.'

'Hello.'

'What do they call you?'

'Malcolm.'

'Round the back, lad.' Kennedy led the boy into a yard behind the house, where there was a mass concrete turf shed. Built onto the side were three wooden walls with a small door. A square wall plate was attached around the top. There was a ladder against the front wall and a pile of timber across the yard, with a saw, a hammer and a chisel scattered beside a long bench.

'Do you know anything about roofs?'

'No, sir.'

'Ever worked with wood, lad? With your father?

'No, sir.'

'Well, do you think you are any good with a saw?'

'I don't know, sir.'

'Pah!' Kennedy climbed the ladder and stood on the wall plate. He took a measure tape from his jacket pocket. He measured the length of the front wall. He looked down at the boy, his shape a silhouette against the sun in the blue sky above.

'Now listen. I can't be going up and down this flamin' ladder all day. See that saw over there by the house wall?'

'Saw, sir?'

'Wake up, will ya! Over there!' Kennedy pointed.

The boy saw the saw. 'Yes sir. I see it.' He went over and got it.

'Now catch this,' Kennedy said and threw the measure tape. The boy dropped the saw and as he tried to catch the tape, the sun blinded his eyes, he grasped, the tape fell to the ground.

'Pah! You won't get on the county team like that! And don't drop my good saw again! You'll bust the teeth! Now measure them timbers there by 18 foot and cut them, come on! Don't be standing looking at me, let's go!'

'Yes, sir.'

The boy took the tape and put one end at the end of the first timber. He unrolled the tape along the timber.

'The end of that tape is moving. If them timbers aren't measured right, Malachy McNee will hear about it, boy! I'd be looking for more of a knack for this work from a builder's son! Measure twice, cut once!'

'Yes, sir.'

The boy put a small stone from the yard on the end of the measure tape to fix it at the end of the timber. He stretched the tape to the 18 feet mark.

'Have you a pencil?' Kennedy said from the roof, as he lit his pipe.

'No sir.'

'And you just out of that flamin' schoolhouse? Did you not bring a couple with you? Is that old Forkan still sending laddings down the Kilbrush road for hawthorns to bate them with?'

'Yes, sir.'

'I bet he is.' A pencil landed on the ground by the boy. 'Mark it with that. Come on, look lively.'

The boy ticked the timber at the eighteen feet mark.

'Now measure it again and make sure! Measure twice and cut once!'

'Yes, sir.' The boy replaced the tape at the end and measured a second time. The first mark was correct.

'Square the line now, boy!'

'Square the line, sir?'

'Pah! Do you know anything? Put the flat of the saw handle against the edge of the timber wheres you've it marked. Draw a line against the smooth side of the blade. It's no wonder your father took ye out of the school if this is the way you do be learning!'

'Yes, sir.'

The boy put the flat edge of the saw handle against the two-inch edge of the timber. He drew a pencil line along the blade.

'Now draw another line on the wider face. Then you'll cut it square. If you follow the pencil line.'

'Yes, sir.' The boy looked at the timber. The sun shone very bright on the stone ground of the yard, sweat broke out on the boy's forehead. Dust still stuck to his face. He thought again of mugs and mugs of ice-cool fresh water from Yates' Well next to The Laughing Horse.

'What are you looking at? Get on with it, can't ya?'

The boy applied the saw to the wide face of the timber. He drew a line along the smooth edge of the blade.

'Ah!' Kennedy clapped. 'I've been trying to get that son of mine to do that for the last year! And would he do it? No! You have the makings of a chip, McNee! Now cut it, we don't have all day!'

The boy tried to run the saw along the corner where it was pencil-marked. The saw teeth kept getting jammed in the wood.

'Put it across the bench! And draw gently. Draw it gently.'

The boy put the timber across the bench. He drew the blade more lightly and more slowly and the teeth began to cut into the wood. He found once a groove was made, he could relax the pressure and let the saw do the cutting. Sawdust spilled to the ground, Kennedy's collie ran over the yard and sniffed the yellow powder. The end of the timber fell from the bench.

'Now, do you see? Hand it up here.'

The boy carried the length to the henhouse and handed it up to Kennedy. Kennedy took it and placed it across the wall plate. 'Fits perfect. Now, use that length to mark the rest of them, they're all that length.' Kennedy passed back down the timber. 'I need about fifteen.'

The boy set about marking fourteen more lengths. Kennedy puffed his pipe on the roof. 'Wait!' Kennedy said, as the boy marked one. 'Is that a knot?'

'A knot, sir?'

'A knot in the bleddy timber! Don't cut by a knot! Measure in three inches at the end and cut it from there.'

The boy looked at the brown circle he had just drawn a line through.

'You don't cut through a knot, do you hear me? Not if you can get around it! Draw a line the other side of the knot and measure from there! Come on, we don't have all day!'

The boy drew a square line after the knot on the timber. Then he used the guide length to mark the end. He cut both lines on the timber.

'Good. Now get the rest cut quick and get them up here.'

When the boy had fifteen lengths cut, he brought all of them over to the henhouse and leant them so the tops ran over the wall. Kennedy pulled them up onto the roof. 'I should have built the henhouse in concrete like the shed. These walls will be gone rotten in twenty years. But I suppose I'll be gone rotten myself by then.'

'I don't know, sir.'

'Well, I do know. Come on up the ladder and give me a hand here.'

The boy climbed the ladder and got onto the top of the henhouse wall. The yard looked vastly different. He could see the roof of Kennedy's house across the yard. A sparrow landed on the ridge tile and stepped along it with tiny webbed feet. The boy turned to the road and he could see the quarry, the men still swinging at the stone, the sound of steel against stone echoing up the road. 'Don't be looking around, will ya! Hold that tape at the corner, come on, look lively!'

The boy took the end of the tape and went to the end of the wall. 'Be careful, I don't want you falling over!'

'Yes, sir.'

They marked all the spaces for the timber joists. 'Now go down and bring up a box of nails. They're over there on the windowsill.'

The boy stepped carefully back onto the ladder's second uppermost rung. He became dizzy at the sight of the yard so far away. 'Come on, look lively!'

The boy got down and went across the yard and got the nails.

'Give me one now,' Kennedy said as the boy came back onto the roof. He took a nail off the boy and hammered a joist at the end by the first pencil mark. The boy watched the nail sink into the two pieces of wood. He then moved the joist to the first mark on the far end. 'There's another hammer there. Take it out and start hammering at each mark. Make sure they are right, or there'll be trouble!'

'Yes sir.'

Kennedy kept nailing the joists onto the wall plate. The boy took up the second hammer and nails. He went across to the other side of the roof. The boy knelt at the second joist and he took a nail in his finger and thumb. He moved the rafter to the pencil line. He put the nail at an angle as Kennedy had. 'Watch the head of the nail the whole time you use the hammer and you'll never miss. Eyes on nothing but the head of the nail, you hear me?'

'Yes, sir.'

But the boy lost focus on the first swing and missed the nail, smacking his thumb. He bit his lip and looked over. Kennedy had not seen. The boy ignored the pain and watched the head of the nail all the time as he swung again. He hit the nail squarely and it sank into the timber.

'Do you want a drink of well-water from Yates?' It was Mrs Kennedy. She had a tray at the top of the ladder. There were two mugs and a large steel jug.

'Softening him, that's all you are doing, woman! I'm working him into a chippie!' Kennedy said.

The boy nodded to Mrs Kennedy. He took the mug and drank the cold water, it wet every part of his throat. He drank again. He could feel it reach and cool his stomach.

'The ladding is parched, John! Here, put more into the mug.' The boy filled the mug and drank again.

'I'll leave it here for you, son.' The woman smiled and went down the ladder.

'These rafters all fit perfect.' Kennedy said. 'You might be a chip, McNee.'

'I don't know sir.'

'Well, I do know. You can wait with me till evening. I might even give you something if you work hard. Give me a drop of that water.' Kennedy went over to the tray, filled the second mug and drank. He took his pipe out and lit it, shielding box and match, even though there was no breeze. The flame shivered in his cupped hands. The boy drank the rest of his water.

After a few moments, Kennedy put his pipe in his pocket. 'Come on we only have one day to get this roof down. Look at the sun beaming.' The boy looked to the sky and could only glimpse the orange disc before he had to turn away.

'As your father does say, the sky is falling in tomorrow. But it'll probably rain anyhow.' Kennedy left his pipe smouldering on the wall plate and went over to the other side. The collie whined below.

The boy went back to the other joist. He put a nail at the end of the joist. He swung the hammer and crushed his thumb again, his eyes watered.

'One day will have to be enough for us to get the rafters up before night. One day should be enough for any man,' Kennedy said, his head on the nail as he hammered.

The boy held the nail again in position. He looked straight at the silver head shining bright in the sunlight as he prepared to strike.

*Singsong* is Martin Keaveney's sixth book. It follows the novels *Schoolboy* (2023), *Delia Meade* (2020) and *The Mackon Country* (2021), a novella, *Caravan* (2022) and the short story collection, *The Rainy Day* (2018), all published by Penniless Press. Stage and screen credits include Ireland's national broadcaster RTE and Scripts Ireland Playwriting Festival. He has a PhD in Creative Writing and Textual Studies. Scholarship has been published widely, including at the *New Hibernia Review, Canadian Journal of Irish Studies* and *Estudios Irlandeses*. He was awarded the *Sparanacht Ui Eithir* for his research in 2016. He coordinates the Northern Writers group which received an Arts Council Award in 2024. He works with hundreds of creative writers and literary enthusiasts annually (see more at *www.martinkeaveney.com*).

SCHOOLBOY

At top of a hill, a schoolboy awaits the battered yellow school bus that will bring him to his first day of secondary school. He is full of hopes, dreams and excitement, sporting a beret and pony-tail, along with a fresh blue uniform. He tries to ignore his tearful mother looking on from the window. He does not know the bus carries a diverse cast of villains, with a catalogue of tactics to relieve the tedium of teenage angst far removed from today's sanitised contemporary world. Available worldwide.

# CARAVAN

Gus Watt has gotten into a bit of a fix. Over the course of 24 hours he meets the woman of his dreams – twice. He is unable to let either down and negotiates the pressures of a relationship with the two Marys with disastrous results. Available worldwide.

'[*Caravan*] offers a rural Ireland full of acute details and nuanced relationships that stay with the reader once the book is finished.'

*The Milk House*

Tommy O'Toole is a talented adolescent from a village at the centre of isolated bog swamps knows as the 'Mackon Country'. He lives in a mobile home with his father Joe, who dreams of completing a half-built house in the field. Nights are spent with Uncle Midnight who plays poker while swilling Dutch Gold and recalling hero stories from his time in Lebanon. When Dad gets caught up in a local ATM robbery, Tommy begins a descent into organised crime. Available worldwide.

# DELIA MEADE

Now the last of Delia Meade's children have married and moved away, she decides to tidy up the little room under the stairs, known as the Glory-hole. Amongst the forgotten toys, worn-out clothes and dusty boxes of photographs, Delia travels through happy and sad decades of her time at 109, Bog Road. Available worldwide.

'An excellent debut.'

*Connaught Telegraph*

THE RAINY DAY

Farmers: young and old, cunning, foolish, greedy, generous, talented and forgotten. These and those belonging to them are gathered in this short story collection, sometimes clearly in Ireland's west, but mostly in an unnamed landscape which shapes those often waiting for that rainy day to come. Available worldwide.

'*The Rainy Day* [...] will really strike a chord with rural readers.'

*Connaught Telegraph*